Changeling Press. LLC

ChangelingPress.com

Shifters in Plaid
Paranormal Women's Fiction
Kenna McKay & Jessica Coulter Smith

Shifters in Plaid
Paranormal Women's Fiction
Kenna McKay & Jessica Coulter Smith

ISBN: 9781605218748

Publisher:
Changeling Press LLC
315 N. Centre St.
Martinsburg, WV 25404
ChangelingPress.com

Printed in the U.S.A.

Editors: Karen Williams, Crystal Esau
Cover Artist: Angela Knight

The individual stories in this anthology have been previously released in E-Book format.

Table of Contents

Ranald's Mate
Kenna McKay & Jessica Coulter Smith

Ranald has resigned himself to a loveless mating with the neighboring pack princess, a lass he can barely tolerate. She's too sweet. Too biddable. And not at all the sort of woman he wants. But he'll never go against his alpha's wishes, and now he must abide by the bargain struck when he and Blair were teens.

He never counted on Blair turning into a feisty beauty, or the fact she isn't too thrilled to be mated to him, either. But if there's one thing Ranald knows how to do, it's woo a lass. His mate doesn't stand a chance.

Prologue

Ten Years Ago

Ranald stood patiently beside his father, the alpha, as he listened to the terms of the agreement. Despite Ranald's wishes, his father was signing a contract with a neighboring pack, tying Ranald to the pack princess, Blair Bruce. He cast a surreptitious glance at the quiet girl. She wasn't what he'd expected, or what he wanted. There was a blonde beauty at home he'd had his eye on, and now he was sorry he'd wasted so much time chasing after her.

Hair the color of fire sprang from Blair's head in a riot of curls. Freckles dotted her nose and cheeks. But it was her eyes that drew him in. A clear green, the color of the forest, they studied him. She seemed curious, and yet she didn't make a sound. Ranald wasn't sure what to make of her. Did she agree to the mating? Or was she being forced like he was?

"Blair, come here," her father called to her. She meekly followed his order and came to stand beside him. "Blair, this is Ranald Douglas. He's to be your mate when you're of age."

She watched him, but still didn't say a word.

Ranald's father nudged him and he stepped forward, holding out his hand. She slowly placed her palm against his and his fingers closed over hers. Her grip was slight and he worried that she wouldn't be strong enough to be alpha female. It wouldn't be long before Ranald took over his father's pack, and he needed someone by his side who could lead. Blair seemed more sheep than wolf.

"I'm pleased to meet you," Ranald forced himself to say.

A slight smile ghosted her lips and she withdrew

her hand.

"Why dinnae the two of you run off and get acquainted?" Blair's father suggested. "You should ken more about each other than your names if you're to make a match of it."

Ranald canted his elbow and she placed her hand in the crook. As they walked off, he looked down at the top of her head. She was so much smaller than him, and he hadn't even reached his full height yet. She was delicate, which was nice, but again he worried she wouldn't be able to handle the title of alpha female when the time came, despite her place in her current pack. There would be challenges, of that he was certain, and he wasn't convinced she would win against the more determined females in his pack.

"I'm sorry you're being forced to mate with me," she said softly.

"My father believes it will be a good match."

She smiled up at him, merriment twinkling in her eyes. "And do you always do what your father says?"

Ranald shrugged. Truthfully, yes, he did. His father was alpha and deserving of his respect, even when he didn't want to give it. Like now. If Ranald could buck his father's authority, now would be the time to do it. He'd always heard tales of destined mates and he'd hoped one day to find his own. Now that would never come to pass, not with his life tied to Blair's at such an early age. The blonde back home flashed before his eyes for a moment and he shook the image away.

Still, contract or no, he was going to have some fun while he could. She was only thirteen, which gave him five years to kick up his heels and explore life a bit. All right, so what he really wanted to explore were the willing females in his pack and the nearby town. He didn't lack for female attention and he planned to take advantage while he could. Just because he was contracted to mate with Blair didn't make them mates already. It wouldn't be cheating, not really.

"You dinnae wish to mate with me, do you?" she asked.

Ranald bit his lip. He didn't want to hurt her feelings, but the truth was that he didn't wish for the mating. It was being forced on him, and in that moment, he wished he were mating with anyone else. Someone with a backbone would be nice. Blair seemed sweet. Too sweet. Despite her attractive figure, her meek nature killed any response his body may have had to her.

"No," he answered truthfully. "I dinnae wish to be mated to you."

"There's someone else?" she asked.

He shook his head.

"I ken I'm no' much to look at," she said. "But I promise I'll be a good, faithful mate to you. You'll never have to worry about me straying."

He supposed that was the best he could hope for, given their situation. As much as he hated to say the words, he pledged the same to her. Once they were mated, he would be faithful to her, even if he didn't desire her.

The future was looking rather bleak. Mated to a stranger. Ranald didn't know what had possessed his father to make such an agreement, but he vowed never to do the same to his own children. They would be free to take a mate of their choosing, someone who called to them and their wolf. It was as it should be.

"Thank you for not denying me," she said as she drew him to a stop under a large tree.

He hadn't realized that was even an option.

"There have been others, before you. Three. Once they saw me, they refused to sign the agreement with my father. I know he means well, wanting what's best for me. But that disnae mean it dinnae hurt, their rejection. It smarted something fierce, and I'd honestly despaired of ever finding a mate. So, thank you. For whatever that's worth."

"You're welcome, Blair. I'll try to be a good mate to you, when the time comes. Until then, you may call on me if you ever need help. I promise to be there for you."

She smiled her sweet smile and leaned her head against his arm. Ranald heaved a sigh. His father had consigned him to hell, but Ranald was the one nailing his own coffin shut. He didn't know what had possessed him to make such a statement to her, but he couldn't very well recall the words now. He'd just have to hope she never had need of him.

Without a word, he led her back to their waiting alphas. The sooner he returned her to her father, the sooner he could leave. The air was suddenly oppressive and he couldn't breathe. He could feel the chains tightening around him and wanted to escape.

Little did he know he'd spend the next ten years fighting the inevitable.

Chapter One

Present Day

In celebration of his twenty-sixth birthday, Ranald sat in the local pub, a buxom blonde on either arm as he downed pint after pint. He hadn't yet decided which one he would take home tonight. Or maybe he'd take both, celebrate in style. His freedom was coming to an end in the morning.

His future mate had balked at the idea of mating him when she turned eighteen. Then another year had passed, and another. Now she was twenty-three and the decision had been taken out of her hands. Her alpha father was dying and wanted to see his baby girl settled before something happened to him. Ranald couldn't blame the man, even if it did mean his life was about to become a complete wreck. All of his fun would come to a screeching halt.

The thought of being saddled with the meek, biddable young lass was enough to sour his stomach. He'd always preferred a little fire in his women, even at the tender age of sixteen. It was a nightmare, being stuck with Blair, but he couldn't very well break the contract his father had signed. It would be dishonorable, and really, it wasn't the lass's fault that she was unsuitable as his mate.

"So, tomorrow's the day," his friend, Camdan, said. "Going to enjoy your last night of freedom?"

"You better believe it."

Camdan saluted him and wandered off to join some of the pack members across the room. Ranald envied him his easy camaraderie with the rest of the pack. Being the alpha's son, Ranald had always been held apart. He was to be their leader, not their friend. With Cam, it was different. Camdan would be his beta once he took over the pack.

One of the blondes purred in his ear. "What do you say we get out of here, lover?"

He smiled at her and gave her waist a squeeze. She was a bonnie lass with legs that were miles long, a sweet little waist, and breasts that would make a man beg. The other blonde, her sister, was just as luscious. He was a lucky bastard tonight, even if tomorrow did spell his doom.

Ranald herded them across the room toward the door, but froze halfway there. His father filled the doorway, a disapproving look on his stern face. With a sigh, Ranald released the blondes and went to address his alpha. It seemed whatever fun he'd planned for the evening was already at an end. He knew that look in his father's eyes, knew it well. It was the look of sheer disappointment. And disappointing his alpha was something he'd done well these past ten years.

"You should be at home. Resting," his father said. "You have a big day tomorrow, or have you forgotten?"

"How can I forget when you've reminded me nearly every day of my life for the last ten years? I never asked for this mating, never wanted it. You forced it upon me and now I have to deal with the consequences."

"Consequences? You get a lovely, sweet lass for a mate and you call that a consequence? I'll never understand you, Ranald. I've given you everything you could have possibly wanted growing up. Even found you an ideal mate. An alpha's daughter at that. And how do you thank me? You piss away your youth on ale and whores."

The blondes behind him squawked in indignation. Although, to be fair, his father wasn't far off the mark. The lasses had been ridden hard and were far too easy. All it had taken was a bit of a grin and a wink and they'd fallen into his arms. But he hadn't wanted a challenge tonight. Easy had been just fine. Until now.

"I've had to cram a lifetime of fun into ten years. Because you saw fit to play god and determine who I would mate. Why couldnae you just let nature take its course?"

"I'm your alpha, son, and you *will* respect me. You'll just have to trust that I ken what I'm doing. This is no' only for your own good, but the good of the pack. Blair will be the perfect alpha female."

Ranald snorted. "No' unless she's grown a spine in the last ten years. The lass I met would run crying at the first sign of trouble. She was weak. Is that what you want for the pack? A weak alpha female? You put the pack at a disadvantage and you know the females will no' settle for her as my mate. She'll be challenged. And she'll lose. Then what will become of your precious contract?"

"I guess we'll have to agree to disagree. I think you'll be surprised when you see Blair again. She's no' the same lass you once knew. I've watched her over the years and she's blossomed into a rare, unique woman. A lass any man would be proud to call mate. You should feel honored that she's yours."

Ranald gritted his teeth, but held back his scathing retort. It wouldn't do to piss his father off any more than he already had. They needed to show a united front tomorrow when the alpha and his daughter came to visit. Well, one would be visiting; the other was here to stay. Unfortunately.

"I'm going home. Alone, as was your intent all along. But dinnae think I'll be going into this mating a happy man. As far as I'm concerned, you've shackled me to the worst mistake of my life. Dinnae expect me to thank you for it anytime soon."

Without giving his father a chance to respond, Ranald pushed his way through the door and out into the warm evening air. Straightening his kilt, he climbed onto the back of his motorcycle, tucking the garment so it wouldn't blow up, and then started the engine. He could see the blondes through the window and noticed they'd already moved on to someone else. Figures. Fickle bitches.

As he roared off into the night, he tried not to think of the all the changes the morrow would bring. To Ranald's way of thinking, his life was coming to an end. No more parties. No more nights out with the boys. And no more women. Just the thought of bedding that sickeningly sweet lass was enough to kill his hard-on. How the hell was he supposed to get it up tomorrow when he claimed her as his own?

Christ, but his life was a mess!

Chapter Two

Blair tapped her fingers on her leg, trying not to think about what awaited her. She remembered the boy she'd met all those years ago. He hadn't been thrilled at the idea of mating with her, and she couldn't blame him. She hadn't been anyone's ideal. Blair liked to think she'd improved over time, but men still gave her a wide berth. Her father had wanted her to go to her mating a virgin, but she'd taken care of that little pesky problem when she'd turned nineteen and realized she didn't want her mate thinking she was unprepared for him.

Oh, she'd heard the talk over the years. Her mate had been kicking up his heels and having a grand time, diving under one skirt after another. Good thing shifters couldn't carry diseases or she'd worry she might catch something from him. She supposed she couldn't hold it against him. He'd been so young when they were contracted, older than her, but still young. It must have chafed to have his life mapped out for him. As for her, it wasn't uncommon for a father to arrange a marriage for a daughter, but not in the pack. A bit outdated, perhaps, but she understood he meant well.

What kind of wolf had Ranald turned into? Despite his obvious distaste over mating with her, he'd seemed kind when she'd met him. Her father had encouraged her to seek him out over the years, but she'd always held back. Truthfully, she'd been enamored of him at that first meeting. He'd been so tall, his shoulders already broad. The way his hair had fallen over his forehead had made her fingers itch to push it back to see if it felt silky. She'd had a crush, instant lust, and it hadn't dissipated over the years.

She'd had lovers, but only a few. Blair considered

it research, not wanting to go to her mate's bed a complete innocent. Unbeknownst to her father, she'd downloaded videos to learn how to please a man, and she couldn't wait to put the knowledge to good use. Whatever her mate wanted in the bedroom, he would get. She'd learned long ago, a satisfied mate was a mate who didn't stray. If they were true mates, she'd never have to worry about it. Destined mates would rather cut off their paw than cheat on their mate. But with an arranged mating? Anything was possible.

"You're quiet," her father said.

"Just thinking. Do you think Ranald has changed much over the years?"

"I have no' seen him, but I've heard the whispers. He's something of a ladies man, but I wouldnae fret. I'm sure he'll be faithful to you." Her father muttered something under his breath and she smiled when she made out the words *or I'll neuter him.* He may be old and dying, but her father was still every inch the alpha male. He took his duties seriously, which was why he would be stepping down after she was mated today. He hadn't trusted anyone to honor the contract between Ranald and her, but once the deed was done, he would be free.

It was sad that she wouldn't be part of her pack any longer. She was not just gaining a mate, but a father-in-law and new pack mates. Would they accept her? She didn't doubt that there would be challenges. With a male of Ranald's standing, she would be highly surprised if the females in the pack just sat back and let him mate someone without a challenge. But what no one knew was that Blair had been training for this day. It's why she'd taken so long to mate with Ranald. Every morning she'd risen and gone into the woods where she met up with Fyor, an ancient elf. He'd sworn her to secrecy, as elves and wolves didn't get along. She'd kept his presence a secret in exchange for battle training. If she could take down a two-centuries-old elf, then she had faith she could take down a bitchy she-wolf.

They pulled to a stop in front of the alpha's house. Butterflies erupted in her stomach and she wondered if Ranald was inside. She hadn't seen him in ten long years. Had those years been kind to him? He'd been handsome as a teen, had that carried over into adulthood? Blair had to admit she was both excited and nervous to see her mate again. She was a far cry from the mousy girl he'd once seen. Would he like the woman she'd become? Or would she still fall short in the eyes of the mighty Ranald Douglas?

Her hair wasn't quite as frizzy as it once was, now hanging in sleek curls to her waist, thanks to a hair mask she used religiously. Her freckles had faded over the years and could be hidden entirely with a light layer of make-up, when she deigned to wear any. She was still tiny, not quite five feet tall, and her figure was… well, her hourglass had a little extra, but she hadn't had complaints from the few boys she'd dated, behind her father's back of course. She supposed she was pleased with her appearance.

Today being a special day, she'd chosen to wear a pretty sundress with low-heeled sandals. She'd even gotten a manicure and pedicure for her big day. She'd wanted everything to be perfect, but what happened next would rely solely on Ranald. He must have agreed to mating, or she wouldn't be here, right? Surely, he wouldn't wait until she showed up on his doorstep to deny her? She'd had all week to pack and think about her future, a future with Ranald. But she had to admit, that several times she'd pictured this day and what would happen if he denied her. It wasn't a pleasant thought.

"Ready?" her father asked.

"As I'll ever be."

Her father patted her leg before opening his door and climbing out of the car. With a deep sigh, Blair got out and followed him up to the front door of the large house. She'd thought the alpha lived in a castle, like her father did, but this home was much smaller than the one she'd grown up in. It was nice and she could easily see herself living here. Was this Ranald's home too? Or did he have his own place?

Alpha Douglas opened the door and ushered them inside with a warm smile. The sound of the door shutting seemed so final to Blair. She followed her father and the alpha into the living room. There was a bar along one wall and a massive figure stood in front of it, his back to the room. His kilt was of the Douglas clan, and his hair was a touch darker than Ranald's. His shoulders were so broad she wondered how they fit inside his shirt. Beneath his kilt, his calves were thick and muscular with silky looking hair sprinkled across them.

Heat spread from her middle out through her limbs; a blush rose to her cheeks. She hadn't even seen his face yet and already her body responded to him. Blair inhaled deeply and the scent that surrounded her was a deep, forest musk that soothed her inner beast and made her want to move closer for more. The hand braced on the bar was large, with long, thick fingers. Capable looking hands. The kind of hands a woman would beg to have on her body, stroking her to ecstasy. Good lord! She was practically mated and here she was lusting after this hunk of a stranger.

Blair licked her lips and tried to get her body

back under control. She'd never felt such an intense stirring before and her wolf was more than intrigued. Then the guilt hit her. She was betraying her mate by lusting after this man, a man who she didn't even know. Knowing he was kin to her mate just made it even worse. This was a man she'd probably have to sit across from at the dinner table. How she would manage it she didn't know.

"Blair," Alpha Douglas said. "You remember my son, do you no'?"

Son? Holy mother of… *That* was Ranald?

The man turned to face her, his gaze skimming her from her head to her toes before settling on her face again. His lips quirked up on one side and he took a long drink of the whiskey in his hand.

"Son, are you no' going to greet your mate properly?" Alpha Douglas asked.

Ranald sketched a bow, his grin turning to a smirk. "Blair. You havenae changed much over the years. I dinnae believe you've grown at all."

The lust burning in her veins quickly turned to anger. "Are you always this rude, or am I just lucky?"

"What's the matter, lass? Do you no' like my attitude? Shame. It's one you'll be seeing every morning from here on out." He took another drink. "Once we get this sham of a mating underway," he muttered.

So that was it then. He didn't want to mate with her. If it weren't for her father's failing health, she'd tell him to take a long walk off a short pier with a hundred pounds of cement tied to his feet. A glance in her father's direction showed he wasn't pleased with Ranald's remark. But she knew her old man well. Well enough to know he wouldn't call off the contract, even if Ranald Douglas was being an ass.

She gritted her teeth, picked up the first thing she saw, and hurled it at Ranald's head. The glass dish hit with a resounding thud, bounced off, and shattered on the floor. Ranald cursed and glared at her.

"What the fuck was that for?"

"You're an ass. You think I *want* to mate with you? Has it no' occurred to you I may have had better offers over the years?" She balled her fists and placed them on her hips as she stared him down. "Just because *you* dinnae find me desirable disnae mean other men dinnae."

"Boys maybe. You look like a teenager. Hell, my sixteen-year-old cousin is taller than you."

"Ooohhhh!" She ground her teeth together. "You may have the brawn to attract a woman, but you're sour and your brain must be full of maggots. You think a pretty face is all that's needed for a mating? I'd rather mate with an ugly man who is smart and kind than mate with a guy who looks like you and has your piss poor attitude. Did it no' occur to you that maybe *I'm* the one making a sacrifice?"

He snorted. "You? You're lucky to have a man like me. Men have offered for you, you say? Were they short? Balding? Have a pot-belly? My aunt's dog is prettier than you and has a much more desirable temperament."

Blair stalked forward, poked him the chest, and bared her teeth at him. "You are rude. Foul mouthed. Too damn cocky. And most importantly... You're an asshole!" she screamed.

Fire lit his eyes as his lips tipped up in a smile that made her weak-kneed. Treacherous body! It didn't have the sense to know he was a man-whore. She waited for his rebuke, but it didn't come. Instead, he reached out and grabbed her arms, hauled her against his rather impressive body, and slammed his lips down on hers. The neurons in her brain started firing, one after the other, as pleasure zinged through her from head to toe. Her lips felt like they were on fire; she throbbed between her legs, and moisture slicked her panties. She'd been kissed before, but this…this was an onslaught on her senses, all-out war, and she was ill-prepared to fight back.

She heard chuckling and it brought her back to earth. Mentally slammed her to the ground. Her eyes shot open and she shoved against the behemoth. When their lips parted, she wiped his kiss off with the back of her hand and took a shaky step backward.

"You call that a kiss?" she taunted. "I've been kissed better by boys who weren't even out of high school. I bet your aunt's dog kisses better than that."

He growled. "You little… Bad kisser? I'll show you a bad kisser."

She squeaked and tried to run, but he wrapped an arm around her waist, spun her to face him, and sealed his mouth to hers. She struggled this time, not wanting to fall under his spell again, but his tongue forced its way into her mouth and his taste exploded on her tongue. Whiskey. Chocolate. And something too sexy for words. As he plundered her mouth, his hands molded to her hips, pressing her against the hard ridge of his arousal. Oh gods! He was big everywhere. She screamed for help in her mind, but her hands disobeyed her and reached for his shoulders, her nails digging into his shirt.

When he pulled away, she was left panting for breath, her eyes mere slits as she looked at him from under her lashes. Passion burned bright in his gaze and she noticed he was just as affected by the kiss as she was. She may hate him, but she couldn't deny that he made her hot. If his kisses set her on fire, what would happen when he got her naked? Just the thought of his body brushing against hers, without clothes, nearly made her fall to her knees and beg him for more.

She was in a world of trouble!

Chapter Three

Holy fuck! What the hell was that? Ranald stared at Blair, trying to figure out how his heart was racing and his wolf was howling his head. He'd been with plenty of women, but none had roused his beast, not like Blair did. The wolf inside wanted to break free and mark her as their mate. *All in good time,* he told the wolf, not that the bastard listened. He clawed inside Ranald, wanting out right that minute.

He took a step back before he did something stupid, like throw her down on the floor and claim her in front of their dads. He backed up another step, then another, until he reached the bar again. Pouring himself another drink, he downed it in one swallow. If he didn't get himself under control, he'd end up taking her right here and now, whether their fathers were present or not. He'd never felt so strongly about a woman before and he wasn't sure he liked it.

Ranald cast her a glance. Her cheeks were still flushed and her lips were nice and plump from his kisses. She looked a little flustered and he felt pride swell inside at the thought that *he'd* flustered her like that. She may claim to have prior experience with men, but he could tell it wasn't much. She was definitely exaggerating her experiences. She may not be completely untouched, but it settled the wolf inside to know that he would be the last man she was with. Of course, that was assuming she was faithful. He smirked. He'd just have to rock her world and make sure he was the best she'd ever had. Shouldn't be too hard to do.

"The sooner you mate with her, the sooner I can leave," her father said. "I know you shouldnae rush a mating, but the two of you have waited long enough.

Despite your feelings toward one another, there is obviously some spark between you."

Yeah, there was a spark all right. He'd be an idiot to try and deny it, but he didn't have to like it. He'd lied to her, of course. She wasn't ugly. Actually, she was quite comely. Even as a youth, he'd loved those flashing green eyes of hers and that vibrant hair. Her skin was more porcelain now, almost ethereal. He wasn't sure what had made him snipe at her when she'd entered the room, but he'd loved the feisty look she'd gotten in her eyes, and it had prodded him to poke at her some more. She was stunning when her cheeks were flushed, whether from anger or his kisses. He preferred the latter, but he'd take either.

Truth be told, things had just taken an interesting turn. He'd been prepared to mate with some spineless, whiny lass who wouldn't stand up for herself. The fact she was ready to take him on, at half his height, was an immense turn on for him and his wolf. They loved a challenge, and Blair was proving to be quite entertaining. He wondered if every time he got a rise out of her, he could kiss her just as passionately as he had moments ago. It would make for a very exciting life.

"Perhaps you should take Blair to your home?" his father suggested.

"So you expect me to just run right home with her, claim her, then what? Bring her back here to show proof of our mating? Way to make an awkward situation worse. Did you stop to think we might want a chance to get to know one another first? This is the first time we've laid eyes on each other in ten years, and we barely exchanged more than a few pleasantries when we met all those years ago."

His father crossed his arms. "So what do you

suggest?"

Ranald twirled the shot glass between his fingers. "What do you say, Blair? Want to go to the pub with me for a drink or three? I think we could use it."

She glanced at her father before fastening that expressive gaze back on Ranald. She worried at her lower lip before nodding her head in acceptance. It was a victory, although a small one. He wondered how many more concessions she would make for him before the night was over. Would she cry out his name once she was under him? Or would she fight against him even then? He'd never taken an unwilling woman, and knew he never would… he wouldn't have to. As quickly as she'd responded to his kiss, he was sure she'd enjoy his touch even more.

But even he wasn't enough of a bastard to claim his mate without spending a little time with her first. They may be stuck in this arrangement, but that didn't mean it had to be unpleasant. Sure, they would sling more barbs at one another… he actually looked forward to it, but that didn't mean he had to take her like a rutting beast without any regard for her feelings. Obviously, he'd already stepped all over them. And yet he didn't feel bad about it. He just looked forward to the next little spat they would have. It would give him another chance to kiss her.

"Well," she snapped. "Are you just going to stand there or are we going? It was your idea to go."

He couldn't help the smile that spread across his lips. "We're going. Ever ridden on a motorcycle before?"

She shook her head.

"Then it seems today will be a day of many firsts for you. First real kiss. First motorcycle ride. And I'm betting, your first orgasm."

She clenched her fists at her sides, her cheeks flushing delightfully. "You are a crass, egotistical jackass. For your information, your kisses are passable. I've had better. And while I've never ridden on a motorcycle, I've had plenty of orgasms."

He put his tongue in his cheek and winked at her. "Sure you have, lass. You're damn near virginal, but dinnae worry. You'll be well-versed in how things are between a man and a woman before the night is over, and I'll wear the claw marks to prove it."

"The only way you're going to wear my claw marks is if I slap you across your arrogant face."

He smirked. "We'll see."

With a stomp of her foot, she whirled around and marched out the door. Ranald followed, admiring the sway of her hips and the way her luscious ass bounced with every step. Oh, he was definitely bending her over later. He couldn't wait to see those globes dance as he pounded into her from behind. No matter how much she argued to the contrary, she was going to love every minute and beg him for more.

She behaved herself on the back of the bike, barely holding onto him, much to his disappointment, and when they reached the pub, she settled on a stool next to him. When she ordered whiskey, he couldn't hide his surprise. Someone as tiny as her, he expected her to ask for some frou-frou drink.

"What?" she asked. "You think because I'm a woman I cannae drink like a Scot?"

"Never said a word."

"You dinnae have to. It was stamped all over your face. You really are a sexist pig. I dinnae see how the women can stand to be in your presence."

"I make it worth their while." He grinned at her.

She snorted and took another sip of her drink.

"Ah, lass. You know you want me. All this fighting is just foreplay."

"You really are full of yourself. I'd love to see the kind of women you've been with. I bet they're all blondes with more boob than brain. I cannae imagine a halfway intelligent woman putting up with you."

He reached out and slid his hand up her leg, his fingers curling inside her thigh. Christ! He could feel the heat between her legs and it made his cock stand at attention. His kilt left little to the imagination as her gaze dropped to his lap, her eyes widening. He loved the blush that spread across her cheeks. The scent of her arousal filled the air, despite the fact she tried to pull away from him. It was obvious to every shifter in the pub that she wanted him, even if she didn't *want* to want him.

"I had thought we'd talk a bit," he said. "But I'm thinking we should take this somewhere else."

She narrowed her eyes at him. "Just because your other brain is doing your thinking for you. He gets excited and suddenly you're ready to go. Men! You're all the same. All you can think about is getting laid."

He gripped her chin and turned her to face him. "Dinnae get so high and mighty with me, lass. I can smell your need for me just as well as you can see mine for you. Your mouth may say you dinnae want me, but your body says otherwise."

"You dinnae ken what you're talking about."

"Oh, lass. You should know better than to issue a challenge to an alpha wolf. Especially when that wolf is your mate." He leaned closer. "You're mine. You may no' bear my mark yet, but you're mine just the same."

She puffed up like an indignant poodle and tried to pull away, but he wrapped an arm around her waist and hauled her into his lap. He nearly groaned from the feel of her lush curves pressed against him; her plush ass pressing down on his wayward cock was a mixture of pleasure and pain. He couldn't wait to get her naked and make her scream in ecstasy. And scream she would, over and over, until the entire street had no doubts as to what they were doing. Hell, he might even leave the curtains open in case anyone wanted to watch.

Just the thought of someone peeping through the window as he claimed his mate was enough to get his wolf excited. The beast wanted the world to know she belonged to him, even if that meant marking her in front of the entire town. He'd never been an exhibitionist before, but Blair brought out a different side to him, a naughtier side that he couldn't wait to share with her. He'd bet she'd be wild in bed. Watching that fiery temper turn to fiery passion was something he was quite looking forward to.

"It's time to go, lass. No more arguments."

She pressed her lips together, as if she fought back a retort, but she didn't struggle as he lifted her into his arms and rose from his stool. Outside, he set her on her feet beside the motorcycle and he climbed on, offering her a hand. Blair pressed her body against his back and he wondered how he would survive the torture of riding with her so close, yet not being able to have her just yet.

When they reached his house, all bets were off. No matter what she said or did, she was going to be his.

Chapter Four

Ranald had Blair right where he wanted her, just with too many clothes on. She kept an eye on him as she wandered around his bedroom, checking out the pictures on the dresser then wandering over to the adjoining bath. He gave her time to adjust to her surroundings, wanting her to feel completely comfortable. After this moment, it would be her bedroom too.

"So." She stood beside the bed, looking from him to the bed then back again. "Do I just strip so we can get this out of the way?"

"Get it out of the way?" He had to have misheard her. *Get it out of the way? What the fuck!*

"I mean, you could just bite me and it would all be over. It's obvious you find me distasteful if you're comparing me to a dog, and the dog wins. I wouldnae want you to have to put your cock inside of me. Assuming it dinnae shrivel up before you got to that part."

He looked down at the body part in question which was making his kilt stick out a good six inches. Did it seriously look like he was going to have a problem getting the deed done? Hell, he'd been hard since she'd first opened that smart mouth of hers. Little did she realize every barb she slung his way just turned him on even more.

Her gaze dropped to his cock and her lips pursed. "Am I supposed to be impressed with that? I've seen bigger."

"I doubt it." He snorted. He wasn't an overly vain man, but he did know he was larger than most. Not only did he shift naked in front of an entire pack of wolves, he'd had plenty of women exclaim over his magnificent cock. But right now, there was only one woman he wanted to impress, and something told him she wouldn't be swayed easily.

She shrugged. "Believe me or dinnae. It disnae matter to me."

He prowled a little closer, fighting a smile when he saw her pulse jump. She could pretend she didn't want him, protest until her voice went hoarse, but she couldn't disguise the sweet aroma permeating the air that was telling him she'd lied. Her body was more than ready for him; he just had to convince her of that. Shouldn't be too difficult. All he had to do was kiss her again and she'd be putty in his hands.

She took a hasty step backward, but he refused to let her escape. Oh, he could chase her around the room until she exhausted herself, but Ranald would much rather spend his energy doing something far more pleasurable. Like making her come so hard her toes curled. Before the night was over, she would be hoarse from crying out his name. She was such a little firecracker; he bet he could make her come over and over again. It was a challenge he was happy to accept.

Not giving her a chance to protest, he slammed his mouth down on hers, effectively cutting off whatever tirade she was about to start. She squeaked and beat at his chest with her fists. The wolf inside brushed against his skin, wanting closer to their mate. His tongue traced the seam of her lips and she opened, letting him in. The pounding on his chest stopped and she gripped his shirt in her hands, as if she were going to tear it from his body.

Beyond the taste of whiskey was something sweet. As she kissed him back, his wolf howled in victory. Ranald slid his hands down to her waist and slowly lifted her shirt. He shoved the material over her breasts and popped the clasp on her bra, filling his hands with the soft, silky mounds. Her nipples were hard points and he couldn't wait to taste them. The hands gripping his shirt tugged and he heard the *ping* of buttons hitting the floor, and then her hands were on his skin.

Christ! He'd never realized small hands could feel so wonderful. Her touch was light as she explored the expanse of his chest and then she trailed her fingers down his stomach to the waist of his kilt. His cock throbbed in response, wanting her to continue her exploration. No. He didn't want her to touch his cock just yet. If she did, he was certain he wouldn't last, and he had hours of pleasure planned for her.

Breaking the kiss, he quickly divested her of her clothes, then stood back to admire her beauty. She might be small, but she was so damn curvy he wasn't sure where he wanted to start. He reached for her again and she took a step back, holding up a hand to ward him off. She hadn't changed her mind, had she?

"I want to see you," she said.

Her words heated his blood. Ranald couldn't remember a time he'd ever wanted a woman more than he wanted Blair. With slow, practiced movements, he shed his shirt, kicked off his boots, and dropped his kilt. Her eyes went wide when she got her first look at his body. The pulse in her throat was pounding and he hoped like hell it was from desire and not fear. There really was a huge size difference between them, but he knew they would fit together perfectly.

"That will no' fit," she said, pointing to his cock.

He couldn't help but smile. "I assure you, it will fit and it will feel incredible."

She shook her head, but instead of retreating, she came forward, reaching for him. Her thin fingers wrapped around his shaft and he hissed in a breath. He'd known it would feel amazing when she touched him, but if she so much as stroked him once, he was going to embarrass himself and come in her hand.

Ranald pried her fingers away and eased her down onto the bed. She looked uncertain, but he wasn't going to give her time to doubt this mating. Whether she'd realized it or not, they were destined mates. His wolf had known it the moment their lips had touched. Even now, he felt his beast calling to hers.

As much as he wanted to feel her nails digging into his skin, he wondered if he should tie her to the bed. He wanted to pleasure her until she couldn't take another moment, then he'd do it some more. The dew between her thighs called to him and he wanted her taste on his tongue. Before he could make his move, she slithered off the bed and landed on her knees in front of him.

Blair gave him a saucy look before wrapping her hand around his cock again. Ranald reached for her, ready to push her away before he came like an untried boy, but the sight of her tongue sliding along her lower lip had him freezing in place. With her eyes fastened on his, she leaned forward and very slowly licked the head of his cock, gathering the pre-cum on her tongue.

Ranald groaned at the sight. Instead of pushing her away, his fingers curled into her hair and urged her closer. Her lips fit around him and slid down the length of his shaft, her tongue stroking the underside of his cock. He shuddered as she sucked so hard her cheeks hollowed. She took him further, his cock bumping the back of her throat, before she retreated again. He felt a small hand curl around his hip and something inside him snapped.

With a growl, his hips thrust forward and he

began fucking her mouth in long, slow strokes. She seemed to enjoy his show of dominance and he felt a surge of lust hit him. He'd always held back with his partners before, but just maybe, Blair was his match in every way. Maybe she could take everything he had to give.

She relaxed her throat and then swallowed on the head of his cock. Ranald gave a startled cry as his hips bucked and he came down her throat. He thrust three more times as he emptied himself in her sweet mouth, then he pulled away. Blair looked up at him with those sultry eyes of hers, licked her lips, and then rose to her feet. Naughty little minx! Lifting her in his arms, he tossed her onto the bed, enjoying the show as her breasts bounced and jiggled.

Blair laughed and leaned back against the pillows, putting her hands above her head. She made a rather pretty picture just then. The scene would be perfect if her wrists were bound and her legs were splayed, a lover waiting for satisfaction. Ranald felt his wolf trying to break free. The beast was ready and didn't understand why it had to wait. He'd let the wolf have his fun, after their mate was well-satisfied.

Ranald grabbed a bag out of the closet, a special bag he had yet to open. When he'd purchased the items inside, he hadn't known why, but now he understood they were for this moment, and this woman. Blair watched him, her breasts heaving as she panted for breath. He reached into the bag and pulled out a long, silk scarf. Heat flared in her eyes as he drew near and fastened her wrists to the headboard. She wiggled a bit, testing the strength of her bonds, and then settled when she realized she could move.

"Are you ready, lass? Read to scream my name?"

"You really are arrogant, aren't you? And here I

thought it was all an act."

He smiled. "Not arrogant. Confident that I can please my mate better than any man has before me. And despite your words, I know there were precious few of them."

She clamped her lips shut and glared at him.

With a chuckle, he crawled up the bed, keeping his weight off her slight frame. Ranald nipped her jaw then put his lips to her ear.

"Do you know what I'm going to do to you?" he asked softly. "I'm going to pleasure you until your eyes cross. Until you forget every man but me. And until you beg me to fill this sweet pussy with my cock."

She gasped at his words and he kissed her hard before pulling away. He paused part way down her body to take a rosy peak into his mouth, sucking hard on her pretty nipple until she arched her back off the bed. Ranald gave the other side the same attention before climbing off the bed. His hands slid up her legs, teasing the inside of her thighs and then he pushed them apart.

She was pink. Perfect. And completely his. The scent of her arousal doubled as he leaned forward and brushed his mouth across her dewy lips. The naughty lass had trimmed so close there was barely any hair on her mound. Her clit protruded and he gave it a flick with his tongue before backing away. She started to close her thighs, but he pushed them apart again, growling softly at her.

"If you dinnae stay put, I'll tie your ankles too." Except that would hinder his plans for her, so he really hoped it didn't come to that.

Ranald reached into his bag of goodies once more and pulled out a small vibe. He popped a battery in it and gave her a wicked grin.

"Ever use one of these?"

She shook her head.

"Ah, lass. You've been missing out."

Ranald turned it on and lightly brushed her thigh with it, tracing circles on her pale skin, with every stroke getting closer and closer to the place he wanted to be most of all. Unable to resist a moment longer, he reached out and stroked her with his fingers. Parting the lips of her pussy, he teased her clit with the vibe, light brushes meant to tease and torment.

Blair whimpered and spread her legs further, an obvious invitation for more. As he swirled the toy over her clit again, she cried out and her hips bucked. He wasn't ready for her to come just yet. She'd expressed concern over his size and he was going to have a bit of fun stretching her while he played. Into the bag he dove once more, withdrawing a bottle of lube and a dildo that was much smaller than him, but probably larger than what she was accustomed to.

"What's that for?" she asked.

"You were worried I would hurt you. This will stretch you out."

"It disnae bother you that it looks like an actual cock? Will it no' be like watching another man fuck me?"

So she wanted to talk dirty? He could have some fun with her, but not just yet. She wasn't quite ready for his brand of naughty, but she would be. Before the night was over, she was going to be his in every way. And he did mean *every* way. He'd already come down her throat, but his wolf wasn't satisfied. The beast wanted to mark her with their scent until everyone knew she belonged to them.

"If you're asking do I want to watch someone

else take you, the answer is no. But this? This is just a toy and I'm the one in control of it. Playing with you this way is almost like having two dicks. Except I dinnae feel the pleasure of the toy sliding into your sweet, wet pussy like I would if my actual cock was inside of you. But dinnae worry… we'll get to that part." He smiled. "Eventually."

She groaned and tipped her head back. "Ranald, I dinnae think I will last as long as you're hoping."

"Oh, sweet mate. You're going to last all night long. I'll be filling this gorgeous body with my seed even as the sun rises. And do you want to know why?"

She looked at him. "Why?"

"Because I'm going to fuck you until you carry my pup. We'll not leave this house until you're mine in every way possible."

"And will you ken if I'm pregnant? It's no' like those home pregnancy tests work within minutes."

He pointed to his nose. "I'll smell it."

Her mouth snapped shut as she stared at him.

He smirked at her as he lubed the dildo. He slid the toy up and down the most beautiful pussy he'd ever seen and then eased it inside of her, pausing along the way to give her time to adjust to the size. When the fake balls rested against her ass, he grabbed the vibe and placed it on her clit. She bucked and pulled at her bonds, biting her lip to muffle her cries of pleasure.

Ranald continued to tease the sensitive nub until she came, her pussy greedily clutching the rubber cock. He didn't let up, teasing her clit even as she came. Her legs tensed and then relaxed only to tense again. Ranald began slowly fucking her with the dildo, watching with hungry eyes as it disappeared into her pussy. She came three more times before he was satisfied that she was ready for him, her body slick with sweat as she panted for breath.

He tossed the toys aside and placed a kiss on her inner thigh. "Now that you're warmed up, are you ready for more?"

"More?" she asked. "If there's more, I may die. I've never... no one's ever given me four orgasms before."

"We're just getting started. Get on your knees."

A shiver raked her body, but she rolled over and did as he'd commanded, bracing herself on her elbows. The sight of her ass in the air, juice from her pussy dripping down her thighs, was almost enough to make him come without even touching her. Pre-cum drizzled from his cock to the bed as he climbed up behind her, hands braced on her hips.

Slowly, he sank into her, watching as she took every inch he had to give. He loved the sight of her pussy wrapped around his cock, almost as much as he loved the feel of it. She was so hot, wet, and when she squeezed him, he nearly saw stars. If he'd thought kissing her was spectacular, fucking her was even better. His wolf tried to burst free and he felt his fangs lengthen, watched as claws tipped his fingers and bit into her tender skin. She'd be marked before he was finished with her, but he knew she could take it.

His balls drew up and he fought for control. Ranald flexed his hips, withdrawing only to sink back into her again. He watched his cock slide in and out of her pussy as he gazed hungrily at the luscious ass on display. He gave her a playful swat and fucked her harder, but no matter what he had to give her, she just wouldn't come.

"Something's missing," she panted.

"Tell me. Whatever it is, I'll give it to you."

She looked at him over her shoulder, her cheeks

burning bright with embarrassment.

"Blair, whatever you have to say, know that you can tell me anything. We're mates. There's nothing you could ask for in this room that would be wrong."

He watched the battle she waged with herself before she buried her face in the pillow and gave him a muffled response. He pulled her head back by her hair and asked her to repeat it.

"I said… would you play with my ass? I've always been… curious."

His eyebrows shot up. He hadn't known what his mate was going to request, but her response had taken him by surprise. In a completely good way, but still a surprise. He reached for the lube and drizzled some down the crack of her ass. As he worked it into her rosette, she groaned and pushed back against him.

"More," she begged.

As he fucked her with slow, easy strokes, he teased her rosette, sinking in up to the first knuckle. She pushed back again, greedily taking more of his finger and more of his cock. Ranald added a second finger, stretching her muscles. By the time he had three fingers inside her, he was sweating and finding it hard not to come.

"I want more," she begged.

Christ! What more could he give her? He looked across the bed and reached for the dildo. His cock stilled inside of her, filling her, as he eased the toy into her. She stretched to accommodate it, almost as if she'd been practicing for this very moment. He gave it a few practice strokes, seeing how much she could handle, before he began fucking her with his cock again.

It didn't take long before her pussy clamped down on him. He felt it ripple along his shaft and then felt the gush of her release as she called out his name.

Ranald took her harder, faster, until he came inside her. As he spilled his seed in her, he leaned forward and latched onto her shoulder, his fangs digging deep and marking her as his own. His cock twitched as he withdrew from her heat, and he slid the toy out of her. Walking into the adjoining bath, he cleaned both himself and the toy before returning to her.

She frowned when she saw him. "I don't get a chance to clean up too?"

"I like having my scent on you."

She arched a brow at him. "Is this one of those deals where I have to wear your semen like a badge or something? Because that is seriously fucked up."

He stretched out beside her, running a hand down her back. "You have no idea how close my wolf is right now. I'm worried that if I wipe my scent from you, I willnae be able to control him and he'll break free."

"An alpha can always control his wolf," she said smartly.

"Except when his mate is in heat."

Her jaw dropped. "I'm no'… I'm no' in heat. I would know."

"No, you wouldnae know. Your scent changes when you're in heat, calling to the males in the area, but you wouldnae notice a difference. Have you no' noticed other times when males paid you closer attention?"

"Well, yes, but…"

"You were in heat those times too."

Her mouth snapped shut. "Is that why you want me? Because I'm in heat?"

He trailed his fingers over her cheek. "No, lass. I want you because you're mine. You're exactly what I need in a mate, and while I may no' have been thrilled at first, the moment you opened that smart mouth of yours I was completely hooked."

Her lips twitched as she fought back a smile. "My smart mouth turned you on? You like being called a jackass, an asshole, and being told you're arrogant?"

"Only if it's you doing it. Besides, I *am* arrogant."

"And the whole pregnancy thing? What's up with that?"

He smiled. "It's just another way for me to make sure everyone knows you're mine." He leaned closer and sniffed. "And for the record, it worked."

She bolted upright. "What? Are you saying…"

"You're pregnant."

"But… it was just the one time!"

"And your point?"

She flopped back on the bed, her breasts jiggling in the most delightful way. He felt himself hardening again, but the look in her eyes said he wasn't going to get lucky again anytime soon. Oh, he could make her want him easily enough, but knowing she carried his pup changed things a bit. He'd never tell her, but it gave her power over him. Ranald would do anything to protect his mate and child, and he'd do anything to make them happy… as long as she didn't ask him to let her go.

"So what do we do now?" she asked.

He kissed her shoulder and rubbed a hand across her belly. "Now we get cleaned up and I feed you."

"And tell our fathers we're mated?"

"I think they can wait until morning. What do you say the two of us start fresh and get to know one another?"

She rolled her eyes. "Little late for that, do you no' think? You know me better than any other man at this point. Or any woman for that matter. I've no' exactly confided my sexual fantasies to anyone."

"Fantasies, plural? You mean there's more kink to you than wanting my cock in your ass?"

She narrowed her eyes at him. "Funny. And yes, there are other things I want to try, but no' tonight."

Chapter Five

Blair watched her mate as he inhaled a carton of sesame chicken. He'd already put away three cartons of food and still he ate as if he hadn't had a meal in days. She'd seen male wolves eat before, having grown up in a pack, but she'd never seen anyone with an appetite like Ranald. She felt a flutter in her stomach as she took another bite of chicken fried rice. A baby. It still amazed her that they were going to have a child, and they'd only been together the one time. Truthfully, she wasn't sure how she felt about it. She didn't know Ranald, not really, even though they'd talked a bit. And yet, she didn't feel like they were strangers either.

She'd never tell him, but she'd been secretly in love with him since the day they met. There had been something in the strong line of his jaw and the intensity of his gaze that had made her young heart beat double time. And then when she'd seen him at his father's house, her body had responded instantly, as if it had known all along whom the handsome male was.

The words he'd spoken to her at his father's house had hurt. She'd lashed out at him, wanting to fight back, not realizing he was pushing her buttons on purpose. It had never occurred to her that he was turned on by the names she'd called him and the way she'd poked him in the chest. If she'd thought for a moment it was a game… no, she wouldn't have reacted any differently. Something told her they would have many fights over the years, if for no other reason than Ranald liked to see how far he could push her before she exploded.

"You're thinking too hard," he said between bites.

"You really like outspoken women?"

"I've always been attracted to a woman who would stand up for herself, but the only sassy mouth I'm attracted to is yours. Any other woman had poked at me and called me names, I'd have decided she wasnae worth my time and walked away. With you, it just made me want to kiss you until you went from screeching to purring."

She puffed up. "I dinnae screech."

"Aye, lass." He gave her a wicked grin and a wink. "You do. But dinnae fash yourself. I like it when you screech and claw like some wild bird of prey."

She snorted. "I'm no' a bird. Birds are food."

"No, you're no'. You're my wolf princess, and you're every bit as dainty as one… except in the bedroom. Or when that redhead temper flares."

"You're making me wonder why I agreed to this mating. If you're trying to win me over, it's no' working."

Ranald smiled and winked again. "You like me well enough, lass. And if you need a reminder, I have plenty of energy to show you over and over again just how much you love what I do to you and how perfect we are together. There are some things I'd still like to try with you, when you're ready for it."

"Be serious, Ranald. I ken well enough we work together in the bedroom, but it's out of it that I'm worried about."

That seemed to sober him for a moment.

"Lass, we're mated. There's no going back. And if you're worried about me being faithful, you have my word that I will be. I'll never desire another woman, Blair. You're it for me."

"Other than your exploits, I ken nothing about you."

He shrugged. "I'm like any other alpha wolf, I

suppose. Trained from a young age to take over the pack. I was popular as a teen, got into a bit of trouble here and there, but nothing too serious. I know I had a reputation with the lasses, but it was always about fun and not about commitment. I knew you were going to be my mate one day. I may no' have acted in a way a mated male would have, but I did the best I could, given the circumstances. I was young and foolish and set off on a path that I couldnae turn away from."

She set her food aside. "And yet, you expect me to believe you're going to walk away from that path now? Just all of a sudden because you've mated me?"

Ranald sighed, pushed his food aside, and knelt in front of her. He took her small hands in his larger ones and stared into her eyes. She didn't know what he was about to say, but she could see the sincerity in his gaze. It calmed her wolf and settled her nerves. It amazed her how a simple touch, the slightest look from him, could do that to her.

"If I could go back and change things, lass, I would. I ken that I hurt you and I'm sorry for that. It was never my intention."

"Ranald, where do we go from here? I mean, really."

"Well, for starters, I'll have to introduce you to the pack as my mate and their future alpha female. And we need to show your father that you're well and truly mated. Maybe we can even share the news of your pregnancy as that should ease his mind, give him some peace before he…"

"Dies?"

"Are they sure there's nothing that can be done?" Ranald asked.

"He's consulted witches and warlocks. Even went to the pack physician. No one can help him. The cancer has spread so far that there's no stopping it. Even if they could arrest it, it's impossible to reverse the damage already done."

Ranald eased onto the sofa and pulled her into his lap. "I'm sorry, lass. Whatever you need, all you have to do is ask."

Tears gathered in her eyes. "Why are you being sweet to me?"

"Because you're mine, and I protect what's mine. Even if I'm fighting an invisible disease."

"Ranald, I… there's something I should tell you."

"We have plenty of time, lass."

"This is important. I realize you dinnae know me well enough to feel anything other than the protective urges of your wolf, but I've grown up finding out everything I could about you. When I heard about the women in your life, I did everything I could to learn to please you."

"Is that why you slept with those men?"

"Partly. But I realized it wasn't enough, so I bought videos to learn how to please you."

His lips tipped up on the corner. "Are you telling me you bought one of those porn star videos that teach you how to touch a man? How to suck his cock?"

She nodded.

"Why would you go to so much trouble?"

"Because I knew, if I wanted to keep you, if I wanted you to be faithful, I had to please you in the bedroom. I knew it was hopeless for me to please you in any other way."

"Ah, lass. I've been a right bastard to you. You're breaking my heart right now." He tipped up her chin. "Listen to me and listen well. You're a sweet, feisty lass that any man would be proud to call his own. I'm sorry my actions made you feel like less than you are. I was a selfish, arrogant fool who thought he knew what he wanted."

"What do you want?"

He kissed her softly. "You, Blair. I want you. If ever there was a perfect woman for me, it's you. I dinnae ken why our fathers came up with this agreement, but I'm glad they did."

"Will you do something for me?"

"Anything, lass."

"Instead of going to your father's house in the morning, could you call the pack? We could show off my mating mark to everyone at once, and tell them our other news. Maybe it will be enough to keep the she-wolves at bay."

"They'll challenge you. I dinnae know how to stop it, but I know I must." Ranald stood and began pacing. "There's only one way I know of to avoid the challenge. You'll have to marry me."

Blair smiled. "While I would be honored to be your wife, Ranald, we cannae get married tonight and I must face the pack tomorrow. Now, we should get some rest while we can."

Ranald lifted her into his arms and carried her into the bedroom, where he slowly stripped her and eased her under the covers, then curled his body around hers. She felt safe in his arms, protected. And oddly enough, she felt cherished. He hadn't said that he loved her, but she wondered if he perhaps felt at least a little something for her, beside the protection his wolf wanted to give. If his beast wanted her every bit as badly as he'd claimed, then maybe there was hope for them after all.

Epilogue

The pack had gathered in the meadow outside of town, but Ranald frowned as he looked out over the gathered wolves. At the last meeting, there had been nearly one hundred wolves, but now…he tried counting again. Seventy? Where had the rest of the pack gone? It hadn't escaped his notice that there were fewer females.

"Where is everyone?" Ranald asked his father. "Should we send someone to fetch them?"

The alpha smiled and shook his head. "Everyone is here."

"I dinnae understand. What happened to the others?"

Ranald's father glanced at Blair's father before giving Ranald a wink. Without speaking another word to his son, he turned and faced the gathered pack and held up his hands to gain their attention. When the pack was silent, his father addressed them.

"Thank you for coming," Alpha Douglas said. "As you know, my son, Ranald, claimed a mate last night. It's been no secret that his mating was arranged while he was still a youth. I'm happy to say, Ranald and Blair have committed to one another."

Ranald leaned over and whispered in his father's ear.

"And it seems the next generation is already on the way. You may notice that our numbers have declined. More females will be joining us shortly. To ensure Blair has an easy transition into the Black Paw Pack, I have traded twenty-five of our females for an equal number from Blair's old pack. They will arrive throughout the next few weeks and I hope you will welcome them warmly."

There were murmurs in the pack, but no one seemed upset. Ranald was stunned by his father's news and he could tell his mate felt the same. If her father had known of this plan before last night, he hadn't shared it with his daughter. It eased Ranald's mind, knowing there would be no challenge for that of alpha female, but his conscience was pricked. Those females wouldn't have been cast out if it weren't for him and his wayward cock. If he had a son, Ranald would make sure the child learned from his father's mistakes. And if he had a daughter, he'd kill any man that came near her with ill-intentions.

"I dinnae wish to overwhelm the lass," his father said, "but when you have a chance, be sure to welcome her to the pack. I've left instructions at the pub that drinks will be paid for by my family for the next hour. Go celebrate the mating of your future alpha!"

There were cheers and a near stampede as everyone rushed off to the pub. The two alphas faced their children, and if there were tears in Alpha Bruce's eyes, no one commented on it. The man was not only losing his daughter, but there was a chance he wouldn't live long enough to see his grandchild. It was enough to make Ranald's throat raw with emotion. "Alpha Bruce," he said. "I ken that you have your own pack to rule, but should you decide to step down, I'd like to offer you an invitation to join the Black Paw Pack. I know your daughter would find much joy in having her father close by."

The alpha looked surprised by Ranald's words and faced his only child. "Is that what you want, Blair?"

She ran to him and threw her arms around his waist. "Of course, I want you here. I ken that you were going to step down when you returned home. Will you consider packing your things and coming here once that's done?"

Alpha Douglas moved closer. "We would be honored to have you as part of our pack."

Alpha Bruce nodded. "Then consider it done. I'll take care of my affairs and return as soon as possible. Perhaps my daughter and her new mate will scout out a place for me to live?"

Ranald smiled. "We would be honored to take care of such a task."

"Are you happy about the babe?" Blair asked her father. "I ken that it's sudden."

"I couldnae be happier," he assured her. "And I'm happy to see things worked out so well between Ranald and you. I have to admit, the way you two were sniping at each other, I was a wee bit worried."

She glanced his way. "I think we've come to an understanding."

"Good. Now, I believe Alpha Douglas and I will join the pack for the festivities at the pub. I'm sure the two of you can find a way to occupy yourselves."

Blair blushed and returned to Ranald's side. Already his cock was rising at the thought of getting her beneath him once more. They watched the alphas leave, but neither made a move. A soft breeze blew Blair's hair and Ranald smoothed it behind her ear. There was something he needed to say to her and he couldn't think of a better setting than this one.

"You told me last night of all you'd done to please me," he said. "Were you also telling me you love me?"

She blushed. "I've loved you from the moment I saw you."

He grunted. "And I was a spoiled, selfish little bastard and practically ignored you. For that, and my many transgressions, I'm eternally sorry. But I came to realize something last night… it pricked at me as I was claiming you, but the feeling didn't settle in my chest until I held you in my arms as you slept."

"Ranald, you're no' making much sense."

"I've told you that you're the only lass for me. What I dinnae tell you was why."

"And you feel compelled to tell me now?"

He nodded. "Before I claim you again, before I make you mine as many times as you'll allow today, I thought you should know that I love you. It may not be the deep love my father felt for my mother, but I ken that it will grow to that over time."

She snuggled into him, holding him tight. "I love you too, Ranald. And thank you for telling me."

"Now, what do you say we go have our own celebration?"

She gave him a saucy smile and began tugging him back toward the road and his waiting motorcycle. "I believe, my mate, it can be arranged. As often as you want, in as many ways you want…"

Gods save him but the universe had picked the perfect mate for him. She was his match in every way and he would spend the rest of his days celebrating life with Blair, and wondering how he'd gotten so lucky.

Highland Shifter's Baby
Kenna McKay & Jessica Coulter Smith

Camdan wanted Lily since the moment he first saw her. One sniff and he knows she's his destined mate. Too bad his father decided to marry her mother, and now she's off-limits as his step-sister. Or is she?

There's only so much a wolf can do. When the temptation becomes too great, Cam knows that he'll do whatever it takes to claim Lily and make her his.

Prologue

Five years ago

Lily Duvall stared out over the castle gardens as tears tracked her cheeks. She'd only been in Scotland a few months, and already she'd screwed up. It was stupid to think a laird's son would be interested in her. Oh, he'd been interested… in getting laid. She was twenty and should have known better, but she'd fallen for his charm, despite the murmurs around town that he was a womanizer. Lily had thought he was genuine when he told her she was the best thing that had ever happened to him. She'd fallen for his lies, up until the point where she fought him off when he tried to get under her skirt.

"Ah, there's the little sis now," a voice slurred from the darkness.

Lily hastily wiped the tears from her cheeks, but not before Camdan Hume wandered up beside her. He frowned at her and reached up to wipe away a stray tear. He studied the droplet on his finger before looking up at her again.

"Why are you out here crying?" he asked. "You get to live in a castle. I cannae imagine a single reason you would cry, especially on such a beautiful night."

"Leave me alone, Cam. I just… want to be alone."

His gaze travelled the length of her body, staying a little too long on the hem of her dress. His gaze jerked back up to her face. She hoped he wouldn't ask, but she knew he would. She was certain he'd have a good laugh over her predicament, point out that he'd warned her to stay away from the likes of Forbes Gibb.

"Why is your skirt torn, lass?"

"Just leave it alone, Cam."

He reached out and gripped her arm, turning her to face him. "Why?"

"You were right, okay? I should have never gone out with Forbes. The last thing I need is you saying I told you so."

His grip tightened on her arm and she saw something dark and angry flash through his eyes. "What do you mean by that? What did he do, Lily?"

"Nothing. Just forget I said anything."

Cam pulled her closer until her breasts brushed against his chest, a chest she had no business noticing as his step-sister, but the well-defined muscles were hard to ignore. He was the reason she'd latched onto Forbes to begin with. The moment she'd laid eyes on Camdan, she'd wanted him. Instant lust had hit her and she'd been powerless to keep her distance. At first, she'd looked for ways to spend time with him, but then he'd started looking back at her with heat in his eyes and a teasing "sis" on his lips and she'd realized she was playing with fire.

"Do you have any idea what you do to me, Lily? I've tried to stay away, to keep my distance, and yet, I find myself drawn to you over and over again. It's wrong for me to want you this way, but my wolf has other ideas."

She rested her hands on his broad shoulders, feeling the muscles tense under her fingers. "My wolf wants you too, Cam. She has from the very first, and I don't know how long I can pacify her with other men."

Cam growled, his beast coming to the surface as his eyes flashed gold. "There will be no other men in your life, Lily. Just the thought of some guy's hands on you is enough to make my wolf insane. As long as you live here, for however long you're in Scotland, you're mine. Just because I'm no' supposed to touch you, disnae mean I'll allow you to be with other men."

"Cam, I..." She couldn't disagree with him because she had no desire to see other men.

Voices could be heard drawing near and he pulled her into the shadows, pressing her back against the stone of the castle. They watched as their parents came out, searching for them, then went back inside. She studied Cam in the moonlight and realized this was her golden opportunity... her one chance to be close to him without censure. She pushed up on her tiptoes and brushed her lips against his.

With a groan, he sank his fingers into her hair and tipped her head back, deepening the kiss. He ravaged her mouth, his tongue delving inside. It was full of passion and fire, and the best kiss she'd ever had. It left her shaking and wanting more. Her fingers deftly unbuttoned his shirt, spreading the material wide so she could get a good look at his impressive chest. His skin was hot to the touch and she felt him shudder under her palm.

"Lass, you dinnae ken what you're doing."

"I know it's wrong, Cam. I know what the pack would say, that they would throw me out, but I want you. I need you more than I've ever needed anyone. You can't deny that you want me too."

"No, lass, I cannae deny it. But if we're caught... you risk banishment, and so do I. I'm to be the next beta and I cannae jeopardize my place in the pack. People are counting on me, and I'm to set an example. We may not be blood related, but as far as the pack is concerned, you're my sister now. This... whatever this is between us, is forbidden."

"I know."

His fingers trailed down her cheek. "You're so beautiful. Looking at you like this... it's all I can do not to take you against the wall like some cheap whore, and you deserve far better. I want to take you to my room, spread you out over my satin sheets, and make love to you all night and all day. I want to sink my fangs into your shoulder and mark you as mine for all the world to see; I want to plant a bairn in your belly so every male out there will know you're mine and always will be."

His words made her body go from a slow burn to being engulfed in flames. She wanted those things too, so very much!

"Dinnae look at me like that," he begged. "I cannae walk away if you look at me that way."

"I can't help it, Cam."

She watched the struggle in his eyes, and knew the moment he gave in to his desires. His head lowered once more as he claimed her lips again, his fingers tugging at her flowing skirt until it was bunched around her waist. With one tug, her panties were torn from her body, leaving her trembling in his arms and waiting for what was to come. She reached for him, pulling up his kilt and wrapping her fingers around his hard shaft. She wanted to see him, to watch her hand stroke him, but his kiss was relentless as he took everything she had to give.

Lily wrapped a leg around his waist and guided him. The head of his cock brushed against her wet folds and she moaned into his mouth as he sank into her, stretching her until she wasn't sure she could take anymore of him. His hips pumped against hers as he began pounding in and out of her. She broke the kiss and clenched her teeth tightly so she wouldn't cry out from the sheer ecstasy of it.

Cam was downright feral as he took her with a hunger and passion she'd never experienced before, his wolf shining in his eyes, fangs protruding over his lower lip. He'd never looked sexier to her than he did in that very moment. He took her harder, deeper, and then she was clawing at his back as her world exploded in a kaleidoscope of color. She was riding the high of her orgasm when her dress was torn from her shoulder and she felt his fangs sink deeply into her flesh, all the way to the bone.

She couldn't stop her cry of both pain and pleasure as he spilled himself inside her. With their bodies still joined, he lapped at her wound, sending tingles through her. When he finally pulled away, he kissed her briefly before taking a step back. She tried to follow, wanting him to hold her, but before she could tell him what this moment had meant to her, he quickly walked away, disappearing into the shadows.

Lily felt bereft without him, but as she heard her mother's voice coming near, she understood why he'd hurried away. If they'd been caught… She shook her head. But they hadn't been. She fixed her dress as best she could and stepped into the light. Her mother gasped when she saw the state of Lily's dress and Lily quickly explained what had happened with Forbes, letting her mother think all of the damage was from him.

Hours later, after she'd exhausted the story again and again for both her mother and her step-father; she was safely locked away in her room. Undressing, she fingered the mark on her shoulder with a silly smile on her face. Whether Cam had meant to do it or not, he'd tied them together forever. They were mates! She just knew things would change now. It might take time, but she knew he would make the pack understand they were destined to be together.

After a long soak in the tub, she dressed for bed

and turned out the lights. She couldn't wait for tomorrow, to see Cam again, to see that warm look in his eyes as he gazed at her. Would he hold her hand when no one was looking? Steal kisses in the shadows? For once, everything was right in her world. It never occurred to her that her dreams would be shattered come morning.

Chapter One

Present Day

Lily sipped at her ale as she watched her step-brother across the room. Cam didn't lack for female attention, but then he never did. Not only was he one of the richest men in Scotland, but the man could wear a kilt better than anyone. Five years as step-siblings and she still couldn't shake the feeling she got every time she looked at him. A warmth suffused her as their gazes collided across the room. The man was lethal, but he knew that, and he damn well knew how she felt about him. Cam had teased and tormented her since the first day they'd met, insisting on calling her Sis even though they weren't related by blood.

Not that it mattered to the wolf pack. As far as everyone was concerned, they might as well *be* brother and sister. He was completely hands off, no matter how much she wanted him. Just one touch and she went up in flames. No matter how many years passed, she would never forget the night he'd tried to comfort her and ended up kissing her until she couldn't breathe. Then, in a moment of drunken foolishness, he'd taken her hard and fast up against the castle wall. It had changed from the worst night of her life to the best night of her life in a matter of seconds. She relived that moment nearly every day, even knowing it could never happen again. But Cam hadn't spoken of it since then, almost acting as if it hadn't happened… it had taken her a while to realize that he didn't remember it. She'd known he was drunk, but she hadn't realized how far gone he was that night.

Cam was a playboy, never having a serious relationship with anyone; so even if they could be together, it wasn't likely he'd stick around for long. She knew he desired her, possibly as much as she wanted him, but he'd never act on it, not a second time. Oh, he teased her about it all the time, whispering naughty things in her ear and trying to drag her off into darkened corners, but something told her he'd never actually follow through. She'd been more than a little tempted to call his bluff several times, but she'd chickened out each and every time. What if he saw her shoulder? If he did, her secret would be out and there would be no turning back.

"You're drooling," her new friend, Blair, said. "I ken that you want him, but you know the pack would never approve."

"I know. It doesn't stop me from wanting him."

"You never told me how an American ended up married to a Scottish laird."

Lily smiled. "Ever heard of Full Moon Dating Services?"

"The paranormal online dating site?" Blair frowned. "Surely you arenae on there."

"No, but my mom was. She met Cam's father and they talked online for two weeks before he flew to America to meet her. They went to Vegas and were married that same week. Next thing I knew, we were moving to Scotland and I had a new, fine-as-hell step-brother that rings all my bells."

Blair tipped her head to the side. "There's more to it. Something you arenae saying?"

"I can't tell you. I can't tell anyone. It would…" Lily shook her head. "Let's just say, there's a reason I don't date and leave it at that."

"I ken you dinnae know me well, but I would never divulge your secrets, Lily. You're the only friend I have here and I treasure that friendship. I'd never do anything to jeopardize it."

"Your mate is going to be alpha one day, Blair. If I told you, you'd have no choice but to tell Ranald. And if Ranald found out, I'd be kicked out of the pack. You know as well as I do that a wolf alone doesn't fair well."

"You love him." Blair looked from her to Cam, then back again. "Does he know how you feel?"

"I can't tell him, Blair. It would ruin him. He's supposed to be beta of this pack when the elders step down. The pack would never allow it if they thought there was something going on between us. No matter how much I love him, I can never have him."

Blair looked thoughtful. "You know, he never dates anyone. He might go out once or twice with a lass, but once he's tumbled her, he never goes back. Do you think he might have some feelings for you, as well?"

"I doubt it. He just likes to torment me. I think he knows I desire him and likes to play games to see how far he can push me."

Blair watched Cam across the room. "Have you noticed that he looks at you every few minutes? And I dinnae just mean tonight. He does it all the time."

"It doesn't matter, Blair. I can't have him."

Blair pursed her lips, but didn't push her.

Lily watched as Cam herded a woman out of the pub, his arm around her waist. It felt like her heart was cracking in half. It hardly seemed fair that he could sleep with whomever he wanted and she was destined to be alone for the rest of her life. Her mate, the one man destined to be hers, could never belong to her. She'd once hoped her mom would divorce her stepfather, giving her freedom to be with Cam, but she knew it would never happen. Their parents weren't true mates, but they were devoted to one another just the same.

"Want another?" Blair asked, nodding to her empty pint glass.

"I think I need something stronger. How about a bottle of whiskey?"

Blair bit her lip, but she motioned to the bartender. Once the whiskey was on the table, with a shot glass, Lily tried to drown her sorrows. If she couldn't have the man she wanted, and she couldn't get laid, she might as well get so drunk she couldn't think straight. Drinking seemed to be the only thing that helped, but it was a temporary fix, and one she couldn't afford to do all the time. Her step-father had settled some money on her for her twenty-first birthday, but she tried to save it for living expenses.

"This isnae the answer," Blair said.

"Maybe not, but it's all I've got."

"You claim you cannae take a mate, but what about a one-night stand?"

"What are you getting at, Blair?"

She motioned across the room to a man that was watching them intently. "He's human, so if you have a thing against wolves who arenae your mate, it wouldnae be an issue. Maybe you just need to release some tension, and a human male is a perfectly acceptable way to do it."

The thought of another man's hands on her just soured her stomach. She knew Blair meant well, but she didn't want to get laid for the sake of getting laid. She wanted Cam. It was his hands she wanted on her body, his mouth on hers, his cock filling her and making her feel whole. Only Cam would do.

Lily shook her head and downed another drink.

"I'll be back," Blair said, rising to her feet and disappearing in the direction of the bathrooms.

Lily sighed. She envied Blair. She not only had her mate but a babe on the way, something Lily would never experience. After her one night with Cam, she'd hoped maybe their time had resulted in a bairn, but no such luck. She'd cried when she'd gotten her period. As Lily thought about her future, the years stretched out into an endless span of loneliness. Maybe being a lone wolf wouldn't be such a bad idea. She knew her pack loved her, but they were the reason she couldn't have the one man she wanted more than her next breath. And she wasn't entirely sure she could keep watching Cam disappear with a different woman every night. The thought of him settling down one day made her want to throw up.

No, maybe that was the whiskey sloshing around in her stomach. She didn't know what was taking Blair so long, but she didn't think she could wait on her friend much longer. The room was starting to spin and Lily knew she needed to escape. Rising to her feet unsteadily, she made her way through the pub and out the door. The sweet evening air washed over her as she leaned against the building.

The door opened again and the man from across the room was in front of her. There was something off about his smile, and Lily didn't think it was just because she'd had too much whiskey. All of her alarm bells were ringing and she knew she had to get away from him.

"What do you say we go somewhere private?" he asked.

"Thank you, but I'm not available."

His eyes narrowed even though the shark-like smile never left his face. "I dinnae see anyone sitting with you, other than the tiny woman who left. There's no ring on your finger, so you're no' married."

"Just because I'm not married, doesn't mean I'm no' taken."

He reached out and gripped her arm, jerking her toward him. Lily was just unsteady enough that she sprawled against his chest. As he tugged her toward the alley, her feet barely stayed under her. She fought against him, struggling to break free. Pounding him with her fist didn't do anything, and she could barely stand so kicking him was out of the question.

"Let her go," a voice growled.

Lily gasped and looked over the man's shoulder at a pissed off Camdan.

The man turned to face her step-brother. "This is no concern of yours. The lady wants to go with me, isnae that right, lass?"

"Cam..." Lily whimpered, suddenly feeling as if her stomach had soured. Before she could stop herself, she emptied the contents of her stomach all over her captor's shoes. With a curse, the man thrust her away from him and right into Cam's arms.

"Easy, lass," Cam crooned in her ear. "I've got you now. I cannae let our parents see you this way. What say I take you to my place for the evening? You can sleep it off in the guest room."

She nodded against his chest and wrapped her arms around his neck. He easily lifted her into his arms and carried her to the waiting SUV at the curb. Once she was safely tucked inside and belted in, he walked around to the driver's side and pulled away from the curb. She must have fallen asleep because the next thing she knew, they were at Cam's house.

Chapter Two

Cam wasn't sure what to do with his step-sister. It was obvious she'd had way too much to drink, and Blair had been nice enough to call and ask him to give Lily a ride home. The last thing he'd expected was to see some human manhandling her and trying to hustle her into the alley beside the pub. He'd seen red, his wolf rising to the surface, as he'd thought about what the man intended.

Sweet Lily never dated anyone, and Cam had little doubt that she was being taken against her will. As far as he knew, she'd not slept with a single man since moving to Scotland five years ago. She'd dated Forbes Gibb when she'd first arrived, but to his knowledge, she hadn't dated anyone since. He'd often wanted to ask her what Forbes had done, but he'd held back. Cam was afraid if he knew, if the wolf had hurt her in some way, he would want to rip out Forbes's throat and dance in his entrails.

The wolf inside Cam didn't play around when it came to Lily. Yes, Cam flirted with her and teased her, knowing they could never be together, especially when she stared at him with utter devotion, but it wasn't okay for someone else to flirt and tease her. He knew it was a double standard, since he went after anything in a skirt, but Lily was his, or so his wolf said. He just couldn't figure out how they could be together.

If the truth were told, he was tired of meaningless sex. He'd tried to lose himself between more than one pair of thighs over the last five years, but it was never enough. As he looked down into their eyes, he always felt empty and wrong, his wolf slamming against him, trying to break free and get away from the sluts he went home with. As far as the wolf was concerned, Lily was theirs, and any other woman in their bed was considered cheating. He always felt like shit the next morning, and yet, later that night, he'd take some other willing woman, trying once more to get Lily off his mind.

It never worked though.

Lily groaned in his arms as he eased her onto the bed. He couldn't explain why, but he'd brought her to his room and not the guest room as he'd promised. He removed her shoes, unbuttoned her jeans, and slid them down her legs. The flash of pink satin had his cock hardening and begging to slip inside her sweet body. Next, he eased the buttons on her shirt free and managed to pull it off her and toss it onto a nearby chair.

His gaze travelled up her long legs, staying a little too long at the junction of her thighs, then went up her flat stomach to perky breasts, and then…

Son of a bitch! Someone had marked her! Clear as day, there were fang marks in her shoulder, and from the scarring, he'd say the bastard had bitten deep. A growl rumbled out of him at the thought of Lily being mated to anyone other than him, even though he knew their situation was impossible. But if she was mated, where was her mate? Surely, he hadn't bitten her and run?

It explained why she didn't date. Whether her mate was in the picture or not, she considered herself off the market, which also explained why she kept rebuffing his advances. Oh, he'd never been completely serious when he tried leading her into darkened corners, but even he could admit that he'd wanted to steal a kiss or two from her over the years. No matter how many times he told himself to stay away, he still wanted her with a hunger that damn near scared him.

Her eyes slowly opened and her unfocused gaze fastened on him. He opened his mouth to demand answers, but she bolted up off the bed and practically ran to the bathroom. A moment later, he heard her throwing up again. With a sigh, he realized their discussion would have to wait, and he went to get her a new toothbrush and a towel so she could shower and sober up a bit. While she got cleaned up, he'd brew her a pot of coffee.

"Lass, I'm leaving a toothbrush and towel on the counter for you. Brush your teeth and take a shower, then meet me in the kitchen."

Before he closed the door, he tossed one of his T-shirts on the counter, thinking she might want something else to wear for the night. His thoughts were chaotic as he made coffee and fixed her some toast. He wondered if their parents knew about the mating. If they did, they'd kept quiet about it. Was it an undesirable wolf? Maybe one who had passed through town? But if that was the case, why hadn't he taken Lily with him? He had more questions than he had answers and Cam wasn't happy about it.

Lily entered the kitchen about fifteen minutes later, hair slicked back, looking far too adorable in his T-shirt. It hit her at mid-thigh and showed off her incredible legs. He couldn't help but notice that her unfettered breasts swayed with every step she took. If he'd thought she was tempting in her clothes, she was far more so without them. There was probably a special place in hell reserved just for him, and bastards like him who lusted after their step-sisters, but it would be well worth it.

"Good thing I've been here a few times," she said as she claimed the seat across from him. "Otherwise,

I'd have gotten lost."

"Look, Lily. I'm not going to pussyfoot around the situation. I stripped your clothes from you. I saw the mark." He slid a cup of coffee in front of her and watched the blood drain from her face. "I dinnae know who the asshole was who bit and then abandoned you, but I'm no' going to let him get by with it. Tell me his name and I'll see that he makes it right."

Some the color returned to her face and she looked almost relieved. "You need to leave it alone, Cam. The two of us can't be together, and nothing is going to change that."

He felt his wolf rise to the surface. "The two of us, as in you and me, or you and your mate?"

"Does it matter?"

"Damn it, Lily! I'm trying to help you!" He raked a hand through his hair. "Hell, even now, my wolf disnae care that you're claimed. He still wants you just as much as always, maybe more so. Care to explain that to me?"

"Cam…"

He slammed his fists on the table. "Who was it? Who claimed you?"

He saw her wolf flash in her eyes and she licked her lips. "I can't tell you. It's better if you don't know."

Horror settled in his bones. "Forbes? Was it Forbes?"

She shivered in revulsion. "No."

"But it happened while you were seeing him, did it no'?"

"The night we broke up, actually. I was standing on the garden terrace, crying my heart out, when a man showed up out of the darkness. He was everything I'd ever wanted, and the one man I knew I could never have. And yet, as he pressed me against the castle wall, I knew I'd give him whatever he wanted, even if it was just for one night."

Her words brought flashes of memories to him. He remembered a garden terrace and a very upset Lily, even thought he remembered the sweet taste of her lips, but those were just dreams. Weren't they? Nearly every night for the last five years, he'd dreamed of being inside her, of marking her as his. But what if it wasn't a dream?

"Lily… Why did you no' say something before now? Why have you let me go so long, spending my nights with other women, when it was you who should have been in my bed?"

"You know we can't be together, Cam. It doesn't matter if you claimed me or not. I didn't get pregnant that night so no one needs to ever know it happened. You can still live your life the way you want, even settle down one day." She traced the wood grain of the table. "I've been doing a lot of thinking lately and… I think it might be time for me to return home. When I first came here five years ago, I never intended to stay for so long. I have friends and family in America, people I could stay with until I figured things out. And, maybe one day, I could find some nice man to settle down with… have a few children."

"No!" He growled, claws bursting from his fingertips and his fangs lengthening. "I'll no' let another man touch you. If you want children, I'll give them to you."

"Cam, we both know if the truth were to come out, you'd lose your place as future beta of this pack, and possibly be thrown out with me. I've kept quiet all these years so that wouldn't happen. I'll not stand by and let you lose your place here."

"Do you honestly think I would choose rank in

the pack over being with my true mate? I kept my distance before because I dinnae want it to backlash on you, but knowing that I've already claimed you… it changes things, Lily."

"It was a fluke, Cam. If we were truly mates, don't you think you'd have found a way to be with me before this? I mean, you're forever teasing about taking me into the shadows and having your way with me right under our parents' noses. But you and I both know it's only talk."

"Is it?"

"You don't want me. Not really."

He stepped around the table, his kilt eye level with her, and the evidence of his arousal not easily hidden. Ever since he'd heard that *he* was her mate, all he'd been able to think about was laying her out like a buffet and enjoying her all night long.

Her eyes widened as she took in his aroused state. "Cam…"

"If you think you're getting out of this house without me claiming you all over again, you're sadly mistaken." He pulled out her chair. "Stand up, Lily."

She rose to her feet, her legs shaking. Cam wrapped an arm around her waist and hauled her up against his body. He could feel her heart racing and knew his was trying to keep pace as it also beat wildly out of control. No woman had ever affected him the way Lily did, and now he understood why. She was his. She may claim that she didn't want him and that he didn't want *her*, but he knew better. Not only did he desire her, but she needed him every bit as much as he needed her.

"I'm sorry, lass. Sorry for everything I've put you through these past five years. I should have listened to my wolf. He was trying to tell me, but I was too busy trying to forget my desire for you to bother listening."

"My heart broke every time I saw you walk off with some woman," she admitted. "But I couldn't say anything. It was better to suffer in silence."

"You'll never have to suffer again, lass. I swear it. I dinnae know how to get around the pack issue, but I'll figure it out. From now on, your place is here, by my side, in my home and in my bed."

He could see that she wanted him and that she wanted to give in, yet something held her back. He waited patiently, needing her to come to him of her own free will. Oh, he could make her want him. Cam had little doubt it would take more than some touching, a kiss or two and she'd be putty in his hands, but he didn't want there to be tricks between them. She either wanted to come to his bed or she didn't. Gods, but he hoped she wanted to. After all these years, he'd finally get to taste her -- and this time, he'd remember it.

"What do you want, lass? I mean what do you *really* want? Forget pack law. Forget what other people will think. Look into your heart and tell me what you want, what you need."

She licked her lower lip. "You. I need you, Cam. I always have, but…"

He silenced her with his mouth, his lips coaxing and teasing until she was kissing him back. He kissed her slowly. Sensually. Cam fed from the sweetness of her mouth, giving her a deep, searching kiss. His tongue plundered the depths of her mouth, dancing and curling with hers. The taste of her was far better than anything he'd ever imagined and he hated that he didn't remember their first kiss.

Cam gripped her waist and lifted her, setting her down on the edge of the table. Her legs parted and he stepped between them, his cock leading the way. He wanted to be closer to her, to feel her heat wrapped around him. When she began removing his shirt, he knew it was only a matter of minutes before he would get what he wanted. His kilt dropped and he kicked his boots off. Her hungry gaze fastened on his chest, then traveled lower. Lily reached out and wrapped her hand around his cock and it was nearly his undoing.

"Lily, love, if you do that, I willnae last. I want to pleasure you, to do things the right way this time. Will you wait here for me? Allow me to get a few things I purchased on the off chance we were ever together like this?"

She caressed his chest. "You bought something just for me?"

"I bought lots of somethings just for you. An entire bag full."

She pressed her lips to his abs, giving him a little lick. "Then you'd better hurry and get the bag. I don't think I can wait much longer. It's been five long years and I'm desperate to feel you inside of me again."

Her words inflamed Cam and sent him running from the room. He returned several minutes later with a bag in his hand. He'd never used sex toys on anyone before and it was only right that Lily would be his first and last. Cam couldn't give her his virginity as it had been long gone before he'd even met her, but this was one thing they could share that would always be just for them.

He unzipped the bag and pulled out some rope, lube, and several toys. Lily studied the items he'd laid out on the table and picked up the Venus butterfly vibe. She arched her brow as if asking what he intended to do with it. Cam merely smiled at her, put batteries in the toy, and then knelt at her feet. He fastened the toy in place so that it pressed against her clit, then he turned it on.

Lily gasped and her hips bucked. He loved that she was so responsive and couldn't wait to see what else she liked. Cam leaned down and closed his lips around a rosy peak, sucking her nipple until it hardened further. When he released it, he lavished the same attention on the other side. Her fingers sank into his hair, holding him close.

"Cam, that feels so good."

Dipping a finger inside of her sweet pussy, he was pleased to discover she was wet and ready for him. Her channel clamped down on his finger and he pumped it in and out of her several times. "And how does that feel?"

She bit her lip and moaned, her hips thrusting against him as she fucked herself on his hand. He let her have her way, wanting to watch her come apart. Her movements became frantic, her eyes sliding closed as she came. Her body trembled with aftershocks, but he left the vibrator in place, wanting to see if it would make her come again. He kept stroking her, pushing her toward another release.

"Cam, I..." She threw her head back and screamed as she came even harder than the first time.

Cam withdrew his fingers, wiped them off on a nearby towel, and flipped her over. "Brace your hands on the table. I'd thought to tie you to it, but I cannae wait another moment to be inside you."

She lay flat on the table, her ass in the air, tempting him far more than she'd ever know. Her lips were slick with her release and his cock throbbed in response to the delectable sight before him. The other toys lay forgotten as he sank into her wet heat. He entered her with a driving thrust and her pussy gripped him tight, pulling him in deeper. As he took her, burying himself completely, she pressed back against him.

Cam's hands gripped her hips as he tunneled in and out of her, his cock plunging into her slick passage again and again. Sweat coated his skin as he fought for control. The wolf was close to the surface, his claws digging into Lily's delicate skin. He entered her with enough force to drive her onto her tiptoes as he took everything she had to give. Cam knew the moment she let herself fly, her pussy getting even hotter and wetter. She called out his name as he hammered inside of her, driving himself to his own release.

His fangs lengthened and he leaned over, biting into her shoulder. He exploded inside of her, his hot seed filling her, marking her as his in every way. He groaned long and low as the last drops of cum shot inside her. Releasing her shoulder, he lapped at the wound before pulling out of her. Cam turned her so that she faced him.

"That was way better than the first time," she said, nearly breathless.

"There's plenty more where that came from, lass, but I think right now we should get cleaned up and eat something. We're going to need our energy if I'm to continue making love to you all night and into the morning."

"All night?"

"You have somewhere else you'd rather be?" he asked.

Lily cupped his cheek in her hand. "There's nowhere I'd rather be than right here with you, Cam."

Chapter Three

Lily sniffed her arm and she couldn't help but smile. "I smell like you."

"Well, you did use my soap," Cam said.

She shook her head. "It's more than your soap. I'm carrying your scent now. I don't think I did that when we were together before."

With a frown, Cam leaned closer and sniffed her arm. With soft growl, he pulled her into his arms and buried his nose in her neck, sniffed his way down her chest, then inhaled by her navel. Lily giggled, not having a clue what he was up to. Cam looked up at her with wolf's eyes and a satisfied smirk on his lips.

"Lily, love, you're carrying far more than just my scent."

"What are you talking about?"

He rose and held her close. "My sweet mate, you're carrying my pup."

Her mouth opened and closed several times before snapping shut. Pregnant? But it was just the one time… Of course, they'd only been together once before and she had hoped then she was pregnant. Now she knew it would just complicate things further. Not that a baby wasn't a blessing, because it was, especially Cam's baby. But now if the pack threw her out, it wouldn't just affect her.

Cam misread her silence. "You arenae pleased, are you?"

"It's not that, Cam. I'm just worried. You seem to forget, we're in a precarious situation right now. If the pack throws us out, it won't just be the two of us out there on our own… we'll be dragging a baby into it too."

"Love, no matter what happens, I'll be by your

side. If the pack disnae want us around, we'll find another pack. Blair's pack is nearby and there's another pack further north. I've heard they have a new alpha and the pack is being restructured, so maybe they need a beta."

"Your family is here," she pointed out. "Your friends are here."

"Lily, my family is right here in my arms. As long as we're together, it disnae matter what happens. I'll face anything if it means you're asleep in my arms when I go to bed at night."

"You really think everything will be okay?" she asked, nibbling on her lower lip.

"Yes, love. Everything is going to be fine."

She cuddled into his side, breathing him in. "Is it wrong that I want you again?"

"It's never wrong for us to want each other. I know we've been taught to believe differently, but I cannae believe that it's wrong to want my true mate, step-sister or no'. I have no' decided if I want to thank the gods for bringing our parents together so we could meet, or if I should curse them for putting us in this tenuous situation."

"I've wanted you since the moment I first saw you," she admitted. "You came down the steps of your father's castle, and all I could do was stare and pray you couldn't smell my arousal. I swear my panties were damp by the time you reached the car to welcome us."

His lips twitched and she gasped.

"You could smell me!"

"Aye, lass. I could smell that you wanted me, and was very thankful you couldnae smell that I wanted you in return. Although, if you had bothered to look south, you'd have seen the evidence. A kilt isnae exactly good for hiding an erection."

Lily laughed. "Then why do you wear one so often? I think I can count on one hand the number of times I've seen you in pants."

"Pants are confining. Besides, what self-respecting highlander would dare wear pants?"

"Um, most of them?" She smiled. "Although, I've noticed most of the pack prefers kilts. I thought I'd died and gone to heaven when I first moved here, surrounded by all those bare-legged men."

He growled softly and nipped her jaw. "You'll no' be looking at any man's legs but mine."

"Yours were definitely the best of the lot, and I couldn't help but wonder what you wore under your kilt. Every time the wind was blowing, I kept hoping for a peek."

He gave a bark of laughter and held her tighter.

"Cam, I know you have lots of experience with women, but is there anything you haven't done? Anything we can do together that would just be ours?"

"Tonight was the first night I've used sex toys on a woman," he admitted. "And despite the fact birth control disnae work for wolves, I've always used a condom until you."

"I guess you've tried everything else... sex outside, sex in a car, sex with more than one person."

"There'll be no sex with anyone other than me, so dinnae even think of it. You're mine and mine alone. I'll no' have another man looking at you without your clothes. As it is, I dinnae like it when they look at you with your clothes on. My wolf was pleased that there were no men in your life these past five years, and I should have listened to him when he was telling me to leave those other women alone."

She placed a finger over his lips. "It's in the past,

Cam. I'm not happy about the other women, but it's more my fault than yours. If I had told you what happened, that we were mated, then I know you wouldn't have slept with all of them. You're an honorable man, Cam, whether you want to believe it or not."

"Is there something you want to try? Is that why you asked what I had no' done yet?"

"There's a lot I want to try," she admitted. "But not everything all at once. The sex toys were new to me. I've never even used them by myself. Although I've technically had sex outside, with you that night on the terrace, our clothes were still on so I'm not sure if it counts or not."

"You want the thrill of getting caught?" he asked.

"I was terrified that night we'd be caught, but I think it's more about feeling free in nature. We have to get naked to shift, but making love outside just seems so… primal."

"How is it no one has seen your mark?"

"I told mother that shifting around Forbes made me nervous, so she's allowed me to shift at home and ride in the car as a wolf on the way to the full moon gatherings, and then I don't shift back until I'm safely in my room again. No one has seen me naked in five years except you."

"Clever lass. No more hiding. At the full moon gathering tomorrow, we're going to attend together, and you'll shift with me in front of everyone. It's best to know now if they will accept us rather than wait until you're starting to show. Besides, I want you in my bed every night and that cannae happen until they know we're together."

She wound her arms around his neck. "Would

you make love to me out in the moonlight? I know no one can see us on your property, but I'd like to feel the grass against my back."

Cam lifted her into his arms and began striding toward the stairs, carrying her down to the main floor and out onto the terrace. He didn't put her down until there was grass beneath them and the bright moon above them. There was a slight breeze and it made her nipples pucker. She watched the hungry wolf in his gaze and shivered in response.

He quickly undressed them then eased her down onto the soft grass. Lily noted that he hadn't brought any toys this time, but she knew she wouldn't need them. Just one touch from Cam was enough to set her on fire and have her begging for more. He smoothed the hair back from her face and smiled down at her. With a light touch, he fingered the marks on her shoulder, both old and new. He hadn't bitten in precisely the same spot, so now she bore his mark times two, and she was okay with that. Anything that made her Cam's wasn't bad.

"I ken that only the males usually mark their mates, Lily, and even then it isn't always done, but I want to wear your mark. I want you to bite me when you feel the time is right."

She smiled. "You know, a ring works just as well. And a ring would keep the human females away."

He kissed her softly. "I'll wear whatever you want me to, but I need this for me. My wolf needs to feel like our bond is cemented, that no one will ever take you away from us or us away from you."

"I would be honored to mark you, Cam."

Cam lowered his head, gently sucking on first one nipple, then the other. Lily buried her fingers in his hair and held him close. Sparks shot from her nipples to her clit and she knew she was getting wetter by the moment, but Cam took his time, seeming to enjoy the moment as much as she did.

He kissed a trail down her stomach and then spread her legs wide. Lily's heart raced as she braced herself for the touch of his lips on her pussy. No one had ever tasted her there before and she was glad Cam was the first. The only. The first swipe of his tongue tickled a little and she giggled, but it quickly turned to a moan as she felt his tongue sink into her channel.

Cam took his time, loving her with his mouth, bringing to her the brink time and again, only to back off then start all over. Lily was mindless with need as he showed her pleasure unlike anything she'd experienced before. When he finally let her come, her hands dug into the grass and soil as her hips bucked against him. She cried out his name, uncaring who heard her in that moment.

"You're so beautiful when you come apart in my arms," he murmured, trailing kisses back up her body.

"I need you, Cam. I need to feel you inside me."

He kissed the bite marks on her shoulder. "Hands and knees, love."

Lily rolled to her stomach and then pushed up on her hands and knees, looking over her shoulder at her handsome mate. He lightly swatted her on the ass, his eyes glowed the amber of his wolf. She licked her lips as he drew closer, pressing his claw-tipped fingers into her hips. She knew she'd bear more than his bite marks in the morning, and she loved every minute of it.

Lily could see the wildness in Cam and she knew it was going to be a rough ride, but she embraced this side of him. As he plunged inside her, filling her completely, she groaned and dropped her head to the ground, pushing her ass further into the air. She felt his claws dig into her skin as he began to pound into her with long, hard strokes that would have scooted her across the grass if it weren't for the hands gripping her hips. She felt his cock swell and knew he wouldn't last, but she didn't want him to come without her.

She reached between her legs and played with her clit, her fingers brushing against the cock sliding in and out of her as she drove herself toward an orgasm. As Cam exploded inside her, she let go, crying out as she shattered. Heat rushed through her limbs and she was lightheaded as everything dimmed but the two of them and their joined bodies.

Cam eased from her and fell onto his side next to her, pulling her into his arms. He kissed her hungrily, growling softly as his lips claimed hers. Lily didn't know what she'd ever done to deserve a man like Cam, but she was going to thank God every day from this point forward that he was her mate, even if it meant leaving the pack behind.

Too tired to move, they cuddled together in the moonlight and drifted to sleep, neither waking until the sun rose over the horizon in the morning.

Chapter Four

"What the hell, Cam?"

He knew that voice. What was Ranald doing at his home so early in the morning?

Cam rubbed his eyes and then focused on the men in front of them while pushing Lily behind him. He picked up the discarded tee she'd been wearing the night before and pressed it into her hands, waiting until she was covered before he moved closer to the males encroaching on his territory. His father looked disgusted, his friend amused, and the alpha had no expression at all. Cam wasn't sure if that was good or bad.

"Did I miss a meeting or something?" Cam asked.

"Blair mentioned that you had taken Lily home. She confessed to having called you and I thought it would be wise to make sure Lily was all right," Ranald said. "She dinnae, however, say anything about the two of you being intimate."

"She dinnae know so dinnae go fussin' at your mate," Cam said. "Although, I cannae figure out why she called me of all people."

Lily tapped him on the shoulder.

"What is it, love?" he asked, earning a growl from his father.

"She knows how I feel about you. That's why she called you. I think, secretly, she was hoping something would happen between us."

"My mate was trying to get you kicked out of the pack?" Ranald asked.

The alpha placed a hand on Ranald's shoulder. "Dinnae jump to conclusions yet, son. I think we need to hear Cam's side of the story before we condemn the two of them. Something tells me there's more going on here than we ken."

Lily grasped Cam's hand as they faced down the most prominent males in the pack. Cam wasn't sure it would make a difference to explain they were true mates, but he didn't want them thinking poorly of Lily. She'd done nothing wrong, had even been reluctant to give in to him. If anyone should take the blame, it was him.

"He marked you," the alpha said, facing Lily. "But one of those marks dinnae look very fresh."

Lily chewed on her lower lip before answering. "He marked me for the first time five years ago, but he was drunk and didn't know what he was doing."

The alpha arched a brow. "He dinnae, but you did?"

"I'm in love with him," she responded. "And I always have been. Our wolves are bonded and there will never be another man for me."

The alpha swung his gaze to Cam. "And what do you have to say for yourself? I cannae imagine it was easy to throw away the position of beta. You had to know you would be asked to leave the pack if you slept with your step-sister."

"We're true mates. I may not have remembered our first time together, but my wolf knew all along. He nearly ripped me to shreds every time I went home with a woman. I should have listened to my beast, should have given in to the temptation of Lily long before now. I'm sorry that I've put the pack in an awkward situation, but I'm no' sorry for loving Lily. She's everything to me, and she always has been. I was just too stupid to admit it."

"It's about damn time," Ranald muttered. "I dinnae think you would ever figure it out."

The alpha's gaze swung to his son. "What are you talking about?"

"Could you no' feel it every time they were in proximity of each other? Their wolves were calling to one another. I've known since the moment I saw them together that they were meant to be, I just wasnae sure if Cam would have the balls to go after her knowing their relationship was taboo."

Cam's father still hadn't said a word, but that hadn't lessened the glare he was leveling at his son. Despite the fact Cam and Lily were true mates, his father still had a disgusted look on his face and Cam knew the old man wouldn't accept the relationship anytime soon.

"I'm sorry, Da. I know you wanted me to see her as a sister, but we were destined to be together. If it's anyone's fault, you can blame yourself. You ken well enough that Lily's mom is no' your true mate, and yet you insisted on marrying her, and I'm guessing you will no' leave her so that Lily and I could remain together and still be part of the pack. You're a selfish bastard."

"All you had to do was keep your pants zipped around one woman," his father said. "And you," he pointed at Lily. "You couldnae keep your legs closed? You had to go and disrespect your family and your pack?"

Cam watched Lily pale and she huddled closer to his side. His wolf was far from pleased with the old man's treatment of their mate, and Cam had to agree with the beast. His father may hold rank in the pack, but that didn't excuse his behavior. A beta was to look after everyone in the pack, not just those he felt deserving of his time. He felt his beast rise within, his fangs and claws sprouting.

Lily released his hand, but gripped his bicep. "Dinnae do anything foolish, Cam."

"He speaks of disrespect and yet he disrespects my mate. I'll no' have it. His job is to protect everyone in the pack, no' just those he feels are deserving. Maybe it's time for there to be a new beta."

His father growled and puffed up, but Cam saw a hint of fear in his eyes. His old man had been a wolf to be reckoned with back in the day, but now age was slowing him down. He was in his sixties and arthritis had started to set in. His change wasn't as swift as it once was, and Cam was certain he could take him in a fight. The alpha was still a powerful man, and was definitely someone to watch, but Cam got the feeling that Ranald's dad was going to sit back and see what happened. Maybe he, too, knew that his beta's days were numbered.

"Shift!" Cam demanded. "Shift or I'll rip out your throat where you stand. I've taken your abuse over the years, but I'll no' let you speak to my mate that way."

The alpha pulled Lily to the side, putting himself in front of her. Cam was grateful to the male for making sure his mate was safe, but his attention was focused on the man who had sired him. Cam watched as his father disrobed, and then kept an eye on him as he began his shift.

Cam knelt on the ground and called to his wolf. The beast rushed forward, fur sprouting along his arms. His bones twisted and cracked until he was standing on four paws, his fangs bared at the older wolf in front of him. Not giving his father a chance to attack, Cam launched himself at the wolf, knocking him to the ground. The older lupine snapped his jaws at Cam's neck, but missed. It was sad really, how far his father had fallen. Cam could end the fight now, end his father's life, but he wanted to give him a fair shot.

Cam backed away and watched warily as his father circled him. The crazy old wolf tried to attack from behind, but Cam twisted, his jaws tightening on the other wolf's neck and wrestling him to the ground. He bit harder, the taste of blood filling his mouth. His father yelped and struggled. Cam released him and then waited for the next attack. He didn't have long to wait before his father tried again, coming at him from the side this time.

Cam spun and his father sailed past him, getting a face full of dirt. The alpha whistled loud and sharp, drawing Cam's attention. There was something in the alpha's eyes, a message that he understood clearly. It was time to stop playing and to finish the fight. The alpha wasn't just giving him permission to take the position of beta, but he was giving his consent to end the older wolf's life. It seemed Cam wasn't the only one tired of his father's crap.

Filled with energy and purpose, Cam circled the other wolf. He saw the look of defeat in his father's eyes, and felt sorry for him in that moment, but it didn't deter him from the task at hand. His alpha had given an order, and Cam was going to follow it. He pounced, knocking the older wolf to the ground and then latched onto the wolf's neck. With a vicious jerk of his head, Cam snapped his father's neck. He dropped the wolf to the ground, then padded over to his alpha and bowed his head.

"Shift," the alpha commanded.

Cam thanked his wolf before pulling himself back into his human form. When he stood on two legs again, he panted heavily from the fight. The alpha clapped a hand on his shoulder.

"I know that wasnae easy for you," the alpha said. "But it was time. It's time for a lot of changes in this pack. At the full moon gathering tonight, I'll be stepping down as alpha and turning the pack over to Ranald. It's time for the younger generation to lead, and perhaps it's time for some new laws as well. Before I step down, I'll announce your mating to Lily and make sure everyone knows it's to be accepted or there will be hell to pay. I'm sure Ranald will no' hesitate to toss out anyone who disagrees Lily and you should be together."

"Gladly," Ranald said, cracking his knuckles.

The alpha stepped aside and prodded Lily back into Cam's arms. "I'm happy for the two of you, but I'm sorry you couldnae be together sooner. You should have come to me, Cam, when you suspected the two of you were true mates. We could have talked and worked something out."

"I'll make sure the pack knows they can come to me for anything," Ranald said. "I dinnae wish for another pair of true mates to stay apart because of pack laws or politics. It isnae right."

"I agree." The alpha smiled. "I'll see the three of you at the pack meeting tonight. Although you're going to have to get over this obsession of yours with Lily. People are going to see her naked, it's just our way."

"She's carrying my pup," Cam said. "I cannae help but feel possessive right now."

The alpha's smile grew. "Congratulations. I'll leave it to you if you wish the pack to know already. Now, if you'll excuse me, I have to give Lily's mother the news about her mate. I'll send someone to dispose of the body."

Cam watched the alpha walk away and turned to

face Ranald. "Are you ready to be alpha?"

Ranald shrugged. "It had to happen sooner or later. I'm just glad I dinnae have to put him down like you did with your da. I'm sorry it came to that, but I dinnae think my father realized how badly off his beta had become. It took your mating to make him see reason."

"Speaking of mating... I need to get my mate cleaned up and fed. Would Blair and you care to join us for lunch later? We can discuss how this is going to play out tonight."

Ranald smiled. "We'd be delighted. The usual place?"

Cam nodded.

"I'll see you there at noon."

When they were alone again, he pulled Lily into his arms. She was trembling and he was sorry she'd been frightened. He needed her to remain calm in her condition. He pressed a kiss to the top of her head, then lifted her into his arms and began striding toward the house. He carried her straight upstairs to the master bathroom, where he started a shower.

Cam lifted the shirt over her head and dropped it on the floor. After the violence she'd witnessed, he was surprised she'd come to him so willingly. He'd just killed a man, his own father, but he'd done it for her and for the good of the pack. She meekly followed him into the shower and stood in his arms as the water beat down on them.

"As beta, you can have any woman you want."

He smiled down at her. "Then it's a good thing I'm mated to the only woman I'll ever desire. The one I love."

She pressed her lips to his. "I love you too, Cam. So very much. I always have."

"Let's get cleaned up, love, and then get a bite of breakfast. We'll snuggle in front of the TV until it's time to meet Ranald and Blair for lunch. I think you need a nice quiet day after the morning you've had. I know the alpha said it's up to us to share your pregnancy or keep it a secret, but when you dinnae shift, they will suspect you're carrying my pup."

"I don't mind telling them," she said.

"Then that's what we'll do."

Cam kissed her again, but held back. It would be all too easy to take her in the shower, up against the tiled wall, but he knew that wasn't what she needed just now. She needed his love and understanding, and some time to just bask in each other's presence. Things were going to be different now. He had a pack to protect, but his mate would always come first, and he would make that clear to everyone over time. He wanted them to understand how much she meant to him, that he cherished her. And in time, they could come to accept their mating. And if they didn't, there were always other packs in search of wolves. He'd wish them a fond farewell and a swift kick in the ass.

Chapter Five

There were murmurs throughout the pack as Cam and Ranald took their places beside the alpha. It hadn't taken long for word to spread that Cam had killed his father and taken his place in the pack. What hadn't come up was his relationship with Lily. His mate stood at the front of the pack, twisting her hands in front of her. He wished he could go to her, soothe her fears.

"As you've all no doubt heard by now, we have a new beta," the alpha said. "What you dinnae know, is that he has a mate."

"And a pup on the way," Cam said loud enough for all to hear.

"Finally knocked someone up, eh, Cam?" The crowd laughed.

"Cam's mate is his true mate," the alpha said. "And all of you already know her. Some of you may not be willing to accept their relationship, and to those people I say pack your things and get out." His gaze fastened on Lily. "Lily, will you come up here please?"

Lily cast a nervous glance at the pack before following the alpha's instructions. When she stood in front of him, he kissed her on the cheek and then handed her off to Cam. The murmurs in the crowd grew louder.

"In the past," the alpha said, "we have treated step-siblings as if they were related by birth. And that's worked well for us. However, that rule disnae apply to Cam and Lily. They are true mates and should be together, regardless of what our laws state. If it were no' for that rule, they would have been together long ago. You will give them your support or you will find a new pack."

The alpha looked out over his pack, daring anyone to challenge his words.

"All of Hume holdings now belong to Cam. It has been decided Lily's mother may stay as long as she wants, and will be given Cam's current home for her use until she finds another mate."

The alpha gave them time to converse amongst themselves, a few breaking off and leaving the gathering, presumably to begin packing. Cam wasn't sorry to see them go if they were going to cause problems. If the pack couldn't accept his mating with Lily, he would be forced to leave, but it looked like it didn't bother most people. They wore stunned expressions, but despite the handful that had broken away, no one else seemed to be leaving.

"I have one more announcement," the alpha said. "After tonight, I'm stepping down as alpha. It's time for the younger generation to come forward and lead us into the future. I expect the lot of you to fall in line and listen to my son. Those who don't will be asked to leave. I know this is a lot of change all at once, but it's time for things to move forward. We've been stagnant too long and I trust Ranald and Cam to bring about the changes we so desperately need."

Ranald stepped forward. "I promise to be a fair leader and to listen to any concerns you may have. If you need something and can't find me, look for Cam. He's going to know my every move so we can work together as a team. Now… who's ready for a run in the moonlight?"

Cheers went up and people began stripping out of their clothes. Cam squeezed Lily's hand and tugged her over to Ranald. He tapped his new alpha on the shoulder.

"Lily cannae shift because of the pup. I know it's

important for me to run with the pack this first night, but I dinnae want to leave her alone."

Ranald nodded. "Stay with your mate. I'll handle the full moon run tonight and you can go with us next time. I'm sure the mated couples remember their first days as a mated pair and willnae begrudge you the time together."

"Thanks, Ranald. What do you say we meet at the pub tomorrow? Blair and Lily can hang out while we mingle with the pack. I doubt either one will be up for pack politics."

"Sounds good." He smiled. "Have fun with your mate. Dinnae do anything I wouldnae do."

Cam snorted. "Well, that leaves it wide open."

Ranald slapped him on the back and then went to join the pack, shifting on the fly.

Cam pulled Lily close. "Well, Lily, love, what do you say we head home and celebrate in our own way?"

She caressed his chest. "As lovely as that sounds, I'm a wee bit sore from all our playing last night. Do you think we could find something else to do together?"

"Whatever you want, love."

"It's our last night in your home. Why don't we spend it cuddled together on the sofa and watch a movie? We can pop some popcorn but will have to grab a few sodas on the way home. And maybe, if you're really lucky, I'll show my appreciation in a way you'll never forget." She caressed his cock through his kilt.

"If that way has anything to do with that sweet mouth of yours wrapped around my cock, why are we still standing here?"

Lily laughed and threw her arms around him. Cam couldn't resist picking her up and carrying her to his SUV. He didn't know how he'd gotten so lucky, to not only have Lily in his life, but to have been able to keep his pack as well, but he was going to thank the gods for it every day for the rest of his life. His sweet mate had done the impossible. She'd tamed the beast within him. Well, as long as no one tried to harm his mate or pup. If that happened, his wolf was more than happy to tear out a few throats.

"I love you," she whispered in his ear.

Cam kissed her hard. "I love you, too. For now and always."

Mad, Bad Bear
Kenna McKay & Jessica Coulter Smith

Jessalyn Delaney has only known pain at the hands of her shifter ex-husband, a coyote who thrived on making her scream. When a brash Highland bear shifter insists she's his destined mate, she knows better than to go down that path again. Except Tavish isn't anything like her ex, and she can't ignore how much she yearns for his touch.

Tavish MacBride is determined to claim his mate and her cubs, even if she's human. The fact that her ex is causing problems is easily enough handled. As a bear, Tavish isn't afraid of shedding a little blood. When the coyote harms his mate, Tavish knows he'll have no choice but to take the shifter out. But first he has a mate to claim… and what a claiming it will be!

Chapter One

Tavish MacBride could feel the woman's eyes on him as his shift began. The fur on his oversize body began to shrink as his body morphed from that of bear to man, a tingle running along his spine as the magick took over. He heard her gasp of surprise and fought a grin, knowing the locals knew of his family's uniqueness, but seeing was different from hearing about it. He hadn't meant to shock her, not exactly.

Human once more, Tavish waded into the water. He rinsed himself in the loch, having gone for a run in his shifted form that left the scent of bear still clinging to his skin. He slid down under the water and came up, the cool water of the loch cascading down his body. A breeze blew down the nearby braes, making his nipples harden. The cool water and temperature did nothing for his rising cock as he thought about the luscious brunette he'd spied on his way out of the pub last night. She'd been something! All lush curves and a mouth made for sinning.

His acute hearing picked up the rustling noises in the brush and he wondered how long Annis would spy on him. He smirked, picturing her cowering in the shrubbery. The scent teasing his nose on the next breeze told him his assumption it was Annis Fram was correct. She was a woman he should have never gotten involved with, but he'd been a randy bear and she'd been convenient.

Music blared, making him wince as the noise accosted his sensitive ears.

"What are you aboot, Annis?" he called out.

She emerged from the brush, one hand on her hip, the cause of the ear-splitting sounds clutched in her other. As she cranked the volume, the words registered as they crashed through his head like a wrecking ball, battering his poor brain.

"So what's the answer, Tavish?" she asked. "When will I be loved?"

The woman was a bampot. No man in his right mind would ever love her.

"It will nae be by me," he declared.

"You cheated on me," she accused. "Everyone's talkin' aboot you walkin' out of the pub with Elspeth Woodford. You made a fool out of me!"

Tavish waded out of the loch, water trickling down his naked body. Grabbing his shirt, he yanked it over his head before picking his tartan off the ground. He shook the plaid out and wound it around his waist, tossing the extra length over his shoulder. He eyed her as he jerked on his boots.

"Whate'er it is you're wanting from me, lass, I cannae give it." He ran a hand through his dripping, sandy hair. "I told you from the beginnin' that nothin' would e'er come of our bit of fun."

"Fun?" she screeched. "I put up with you stickin' your paws all o'er me for the last three months. I had lunch with your insane mother! Chief or nae, you're nae half the man your brother is."

He grinned, having a fair idea which brother she meant. Quinn and Gavan had called her a fortune-hunting whore. That left Calder, the youngest of the MacBride boys, who didn't seem to care where he stuck his cock as long as he was well-satisfied in the end.

"If Calder is showin' you such a good time, dinnae let me stand in your way."

"Get it right up ye, Tavish MacBride! I'll nae waste another moment on you."

Tavish's grin widened as he watched her storm

off, the Linda Ronstadt song still blaring. He wondered how far she'd get before she turned the blasted thing off. As if a few lyrics would make him declare himself? He snorted. He'd known from the first she wasn't his mate, and he wasn't about to settle for anything less. Bears mated for life, and he wasn't about to stick himself with the likes of her.

Picking his keys up off the ground, Tavish began walking back toward his truck. If Annis was out of his life without him having to be an ass, then all was right in his world. While it was true he had stepped outside of the pub with Elspeth, he hadn't taken her to his bed. She'd had a rough night, having just broken up with her boyfriend, and he'd offered her the comfort only a friend could give. He'd known the lass since she was in diapers and he wouldn't turn his back on her regardless of what people thought.

Not that his arrangement with Annis had stopped him from sleeping with other women, ones he didn't consider friends. Tavish hadn't had anything serious with the redhead, so he didn't owe her fidelity. She sure as hell hadn't been faithful to him. If the murmurs around town were true, Calder wasn't the first man she'd taken to her bed since linking herself to Tavish. She wanted the prestige of being a clan chief's wife, and the money that went with it. The small castle he owned probably had something to with it as well, now that he thought about it. But apparently what she didn't want was him. "Good riddance," he muttered as he drove home.

He found it humorous Annis thought his mother was crazy, especially since his mother had said much the same about her. He hadn't wanted the two to meet, but his mother had insisted once she heard he'd been seen around town with Annis on several occasions.

Tavish knew it wouldn't have mattered if Annis wasn't crazy. His mother still wouldn't have liked her. No one was good enough for her favorite son and alpha of their clan.

As an alpha, his wife needed to be strong, yet compassionate. She'd have to get along well with others in order to help lead by his side. He needed someone quick on her feet with creative solutions to problems. Those were all the qualities his clan needed in his mate. What *he* wanted was a beautiful woman who wouldn't kick him out of bed. But then, he had yet to meet a woman who didn't welcome him with open arms. He liked to think of it as practice. The more women he pleased, the better equipped he'd be to please his mate. Although he wasn't entirely certain she would see it that way.

Tavish pulled down his long drive and parked in front of his home. Women always found it strange that he didn't drive something flashier, like a Mercedes, but he liked his truck, even if it did look out of place parked in front of his castle. He jogged up the steps and went through the front door, closing it behind him, the sound echoing through the front entry and up the grand staircase.

"Tavish?" his mother called out, appearing from the sitting room on the right. "I thought that might be you."

"Did you need something, Mother?"

"I was wonderin' when you might bring that girlfriend of yours around for a family dinner."

Tavish smiled. "I dinnae have a girlfriend, nae anymore. She informed me today that she wanted nothin' more to do with me."

He saw the gleam in his mother's eye as she fought to keep her expression neutral. The old bat was thrilled with the news, but she wasn't about to let on.

"Oh, dear. And I had so hoped I could get to know her a bit better."

His smile broadened. "You're a rotten liar, Mother. You dinnae like her any more than she liked you."

His mother snorted. "Everyone likes me."

Everyone tolerated her was more like it, but Tavish loved her dearly and wouldn't change her for anything. Even if she did like to meddle in his life. Now that she knew he was unattached again, she'd begin parading sows under his nose as if he hadn't already seen every available woman within a three-town radius. She'd have to find a bigger pool to play in if she was going to find his mate.

"Where are the boys?" he asked.

"Your brothers are around somewhere, probably eatin' everythin' in the pantry."

"I'll try the kitchen then." He leaned down to kiss his mother on the cheek before progressing through the house, taking one turn after another, until he found himself in the comfort of the kitchen, the warmest, best-smelling room in the house.

"Alpha," Rhona said. "Is there somethin' I can help you with?"

"Nae at the moment, Rhona. Unless you've seen my brothers?"

The housekeeper shook her head. "Nae since this morn. Calder said he had plans and the other two went off together. Probably causin' mischief, the lot of them. Why you dinnae put a tighter leash on them I dinnae ken. One of these days, some poor girl is goin' to end up on your doorstep with a babe in her belly from one of those three."

He folded his arms over his chest. "It could just

as easily happen to me."

Rhona shook her head. "You're too careful for that. But those three? They dinnae always think with their heads." She snorted. "Nae the ones attached to their necks anyway."

Tavish couldn't help but laugh, the booming sound ricocheting off the walls.

"I'll have a talk with them, Rhona, but I dinnae think it will do any good. They are set in their ways and determined to have a bit of fun before settlin' down with their mates. They'll fall, one after the other, when the time is right. Just you wait and see."

She sighed. "I'd just be happy to live long enough to see you settled, Alpha. Would it nae be nice to have wee ones in the house again? A future alpha to follow in your footsteps?"

"I'm nae in a hurry to set up my nursery, Rhona, but if my mate comes along, I will welcome her with open arms. I think aboot her from time to time, wonder what she looks like, if she's sweet. Gods save me if I end up with someone like Annis. I'd go mad within a week."

"Wheesht. Dinnae e'en mention that one. She's rotten from the inside out. I dinnae know what you saw in her, other than a pretty face. But mark my words, Alpha, beauty fades o'er time, but a good woman will always be a good woman."

He smiled. "I'll keep it in mind, Rhona."

"You'll want to keep your shiftin' to a minimum the next few weeks. I've heard there's a group of Americans come to visit. Dougal at the pub said they arrived yesterday. It's lucky you weren't caught earlier."

"I'll try to keep my bear tucked away until they're gone," he promised.

She nodded. "Cook is making your favorite tonight, so try nae to be late. You know how grumpy she gets when she has to hold the meal."

"Aye, I ken it well. I'll find my brothers and bring them home. Probably down at the pub, if I know the three of them."

He kissed Rhona's weathered cheek and went in search of his wayward, mischief-making brothers. He wouldn't be the least surprised to find them on their fourth round at the pub, each with a woman in their lap. They were good men, all of them, but when it came to the fairer sex they could be a little misguided.

As he parked outside the pub, he tucked his keys inside his plaid and prepared himself for the worst. If Annis had stormed off to lick her wounds, there was a good chance she was with Calder. Not that Tavish cared, but the lass would want someone to make her feel wanted. While he'd be content to never see the woman again, he knew he wouldn't get off that easy. She was a venomous snake and would strike out at him for the slight she felt, probably using his other brothers to try to make him jealous.

The door to the pub swung open and Tavish stepped into the dim interior. Just as he'd thought, all three brothers were lined up at the bar, not lacking for female attention. If he were to join them, he knew it would only be a matter of time before the women flocked to him. He'd never minded being an eligible bachelor, because it had meant getting all the pussy he wanted, but now that he was getting older he wasn't as satisfied with his life as he'd once been.

Knowing he would come to regret it, he slid onto the barstool next to Quinn and motioned to the bartender for a pint. He'd come all this way, he might as well enjoy himself a little. No harm ever came from a few drinks.

As he turned to face the room, a scent teased his nose, soft and sweet. He scanned the interior of the pub, taking in every patron, until he found her. The brunette from the previous night. She sat at a table with her friends in the corner, but half her face lay in shadows. She seemed upset and the bear inside him poked and prodded him, urging him to check on her. The rotten beast hadn't shown so much interest in a woman before and it piqued Tavish's curiosity.

He leaned closer to Quinn. "What do you ken of the brunette in the corner?"

Quinn turned and followed the direction of Tavish's gaze. "She was already here with her group of friends when we arrived a half hour ago. They have swarmed around her for some reason and will nae let her out of their sight. Why?"

"My bear wants me to go meet her."

Quinn cocked an eyebrow. "Your bear, eh? Are you sure it's your bear who's interested and nae your cock? She's a fine lookin' woman."

Tavish snarled at him.

Quinn merely smirked back and waved a hand toward the table of women. "By all means, Alpha. She's all yours."

Tavish rose from his stool and made his way through the pub to the back corner. When he approached their table, bits and pieces of their whispered words caught his attention, but he couldn't make sense of them. With a smile firmly in place, he stopped next to the woman who had piqued his bear's interest.

"Lass," he said, hoping to get her attention.

When she looked up at him with eyes full of pain and heartache, the words died on his lips. He hunkered down next to her, taking her chin in his hand, turning her face toward the light. The bruise forming on her cheek had him cursing and heat flooding through him as he fought the urge to tear something apart.

"What happened, lass? Who did this to you?" he asked.

"We don't need your help," one of her friends said, a hand on her hip. "Just go back to your buddies at the bar. If you're looking for a quick lay, you won't find it here."

He held her steady gaze, his hand still gently holding the chin of the beautiful creature he wanted to know better. "I'll nae hurt her. I want to help."

"You can't help me," the battered woman said. "No one can."

Chapter Two

Jess didn't know why she'd thought she could escape. Eighteen years of marriage, of torment and fear, and she'd thought she was finally free. But could he let her go? No. It wasn't enough that he'd dragged things out and not signed the divorce papers for months, but now he'd followed her to Scotland. It had sounded so simple. Take a trip with her girlfriends to get away for a while, leave the kids at home with the grandparents, but it was fast turning into a nightmare.

Nicholas didn't seem to have any interest in the kids, even though they'd seen their fair share of his special kind of attention over the years. She didn't understand why he wanted her back. Love had been missing from their marriage for a long time, if it had ever truly existed. All he did was belittle her, and that was on a good day. The other days he let his fists do the talking.

She felt the Scotsman approach, had noticed him the previous night, but the last thing she needed was a hookup. Men were the bane of her existence and she was much better off without one, right? Maybe if she found a nice man someday, one who would treat her kids like they were his own, then maybe she could see herself giving love another try. Too bad there wasn't some magical way to know you were destined to be with someone.

"Lass."

She refused to look up at him. If she ignored him, would he go back to the bar?

Gently, he pinched her chin between his large fingers and turned her to face him. She saw the concern and anger in his eyes when he noticed the bruise on her cheek. It wasn't like she could hide it.

"What happened, lass? Who did this to you?" he asked.

"We don't need your help," her friend Monica said, a hand on her hip. "Just go back to your buddies at the bar. If you're looking for a quick lay, you won't find it here."

The Scotsman held her steady gaze, his hand still gently holding her chin. "I'll nae hurt her. I want to help."

"You can't help me," Jess said. "No one can."

"Now, lass. That cannae be true. I swear it, if you tell me who did this to you, I'll see you avenged."

Her eyes widened a little. "Avenged? What exactly does that mean?"

She had visions of a sword-swinging barbarian going after Nicholas, which almost made her smile. She'd love to see the look on his face if this huge Highlander went after him with a claymore. Her lips twitched.

"Ah, that was almost a smile there, lass." His lips tipped up on the corners and her breath stilled. She couldn't remember ever seeing a more handsome man before. What he was doing at her table she didn't understand. "Tell me his name, lass. I ken just aboot everyone in this town. You tell me who's responsible and I'll see that justice is done."

Monica snorted. "Yeah, because she wants a club-wielding caveman to beat up her ex. On second thought, that isn't such a bad idea."

"Ex?" the Scotsman asked.

"Her asshole of an ex-husband followed her to Scotland. It's his handiwork you see on her face. I guess we should just be grateful he didn't do worse." She muttered something he didn't quite catch. "I never thought he'd leave the US just to get his hands on her."

Jess saw his eyes flare, then change from a mossy green to a golden brown, then back again. She thought it was just her imagination playing tricks on her until it happened again. Through the hand gripping her chin, she felt a tremor rake his body, as if he were trying to contain something within himself. Could he be like her ex? Were there others out there like him? The man was huge, and if he also had a shifter's strength, she wouldn't stand a chance. Yet, he'd seemed enraged by what Nicholas had done to her. Was it possible it wasn't her ex's shifter side that had made him so violent?

The Scot looked at Monica. "Do you have a picture of this ex? Do you ken where he's stayin'?"

Monica snatched Jess's phone off the table and began scrolling through the photo gallery. When she found what she was looking for, she flipped the phone around and showed the Scot the last family picture with Nicholas. Jess had meant to delete it, but the kids looked so happy in the photo she hadn't been able to part with it.

The Scot looked from the picture to Jess. "Are those your kids?"

She nodded. "Piper is sixteen and Donovan is thirteen. You'd think it was the other way around, as tall as he is."

"Your ex disnae look verra tall."

Jess smiled. "He isn't. The men on my side of the family are all over six feet tall. Donovan took after them."

"I don't know where the asshole is staying," Monica said. "We're at the Sheep's Heid Inn and it wouldn't surprise me at all if he'd found a room at the same place. The better to keep an eye on Jess and ensure she doesn't have any fun."

The Scot waved toward the phone. "May I borrow that for a moment?"

Monica arched a brow, but handed the phone over. The Scot rose to his feet and returned to the three men he'd been sitting with. Jess watched as they talked amongst themselves and didn't miss the dark looks cast her way. When he returned, the men followed him.

The Scot handed the phone back to Monica and knelt in front of Jess again, taking her hand in his. The way his fingers wrapped around her smaller hand, the callused feel of them against her softer skin, sent shivers down her spine. There was heat in his touch, something she'd only ever read about. She watched his eyes do that weird thing again where they changed colors, and it was on the tip of her tongue to ask him about it.

"Lass, these are my brothers. Quinn, Gavan, and Calder. We've discussed it and until the situation with your ex is sorted, we think it would be best if your friends and you were to stay at the castle with us."

"Castle?" Jess asked. Maybe her brain was muddled from his nearness, but he wasn't making any sense. Did he mean that he lived in a castle?

"Aye." He smiled. "Perhaps I should start by introducin' myself. I'm Tavish MacBride, Chief of the MacBride clan. I live with my family in Balmare Castle just outside of town."

Outside of town? As in, away from everyone else? Did she look desperate enough to run off with a complete stranger to hide away in his castle -- assuming there even was a castle? What if he was an ax murderer? Even worse, what if this was all a game and he knew Nicholas, and it was a ploy to isolate her even more?

"Thank you," she forced out. "But I think we're better off at the inn."

A low rumble came from deep within his chest and his eyes flashed golden brown again. "Lass, I'm nae goin' to hurt you. I want to protect you, and I cannae do that if you arenae within reach. If it makes you feel any better, my mother lives in the castle with us."

"Your mother?" she asked.

He nodded. "Would you like to meet her, lass? She disnae normally come to the pub, but I'm sure she'd make an exception this one time."

Ax murderers didn't ask you to meet their mothers, did they?

"How do we know you're any better than Nicholas?" Monica asked, arms folded over her chest. "Just because you say you want to help doesn't mean you will. Like I said, if you're looking to get laid, you came to the wrong table."

"I'm nae lookin' to get laid, as you put it. I noticed your friend last night," he told Monica. "When I came o'er to introduce myself, I'd thought to ask her out for dinner."

"Sure, because men are so noble," Monica said.

Tavish sighed and looked back at Jess. "Lass, I ken you've been ill-used during the time of your marriage, but nae all men are like your Nicholas. Some of us ken how to treat a woman, and it isnae by usin' our fists on her."

"Tavish is well respected around here," Quinn said. "Let him help you. If nothin' else, he can keep you safe until your ex goes away. Nicholas will nae be able to get on castle grounds, and one of us can escort you when you want to go out."

A growl rumbled out of Tavish again, making

Jess's eyes go wide.

"Easy, brother," Quinn said, placing his hand on Tavish's shoulder. "We ken she means somethin' to you, and we only mean to help."

The Scot's eyes hadn't changed back and were still golden brown. She swallowed down her fear and stared at him. The hand holding hers made her feel strange things, made her want things she'd once dreamed of but had long forgotten. Did she dare put her trust in another man? Last time it had damn near killed her and had definitely ruined her life. She'd bear the scars from Nicholas for years to come, both physical and emotional. And her poor kids! She was a horrible mother to have stayed with him for so long, but she'd been scared.

"What's it to be, lass?" Tavish asked. "Will you come with us?"

"I-I don't know." She looked up at Monica for some sign as to what she should do. Obviously, she didn't know a good man when she saw one, or she would have never ended up with Nicholas. If she'd been fooled once, she could be fooled again.

Monica studied the men before returning her gaze to Jess. "I say we give them a chance. If they can chase off Nicholas, that makes them okay in my book. And it isn't like he's asking you to run off with him alone. He invited all of us."

Jess looked at her friends gathered near her.

"All right," she said, looking back at the Scotsman. "We'll go with you."

He gave her a broad smile before standing. With a gentle tug on her hand, he helped her to her feet and looped her arm through his. "Allow me to take you back to the inn so you can gather your things. Your friends can follow in their car, or my brothers can take them."

"We walked," Jess said.

"Then my brothers would be happy to drive them."

Jess swallowed down her trepidation over being alone with the big Scot and followed him out to his truck. The sun from the morning had disappeared behind ominous clouds, and a shudder went through Jess as she thought of the impending storm. She'd once loved storms but Nicholas had always used them against her, ruining the beauty of them for her.

"Are you all right, lass?" Tavish asked. He wrapped an arm around her waist and pulled her close against his body. If she'd thought the simple touch in the pub was electrifying, this one was downright sinful. She felt the heat of him pressed against her, the span of his hand on her hip. It made her wish for things she had no business wishing for. She was the mother of a nearly grown child. The fanciful thoughts running through her head were better suited to a girl on the verge of womanhood, not someone thirty-six and divorced with kids. She should know better than to dream of knights on white steeds.

Once she was safely buckled into the truck, Tavish closed the door and stopped to talk with his brothers for a moment. He slid behind the wheel and pulled away from the pub.

"Shouldn't we wait for them?" Jess asked, looking out the back window at her friends.

"They'll be along shortly. Your friend, Monica, offered to pack your things for you. We thought it best if you dinnae return to the inn, just in case Nicholas is there. My brothers will bring them and all your belongings to the castle just as soon as they're done. Dinnae worry, lass. Everythin' will be fine."

She wished she could believe him, but deep in her gut she knew Nicholas would come for her no matter where she went. He'd hounded her since the divorce, but she had no proof that he'd been stalking her. She'd tried going to the police and they had brushed her off. Jess wondered if it had anything to do with Nicholas having friends on the police force. The police liked to give the firemen a hard time, but when it came down to it they all stuck together. She still didn't know how Nicholas had gotten away from the fire station on such short notice. She hadn't informed him of her trip until last week, and that was only as a courtesy so he'd know where to go to visit the kids.

"You're thinkin' awfully hard o'er there, lass. When you see the castle, you'll feel better. It has a strong wall surrounding it and you cannae enter without the gate code. I'll make sure security knows nae to allow any American males on the grounds until we have your Nicholas taken care of."

Taken care of... Jess wasn't sure what he meant by that, and she wasn't sure she wanted to know. If something bad were to happen to Nicholas, she certainly wouldn't spill tears over him. He'd made her life a living hell since the day they'd gotten married. She hadn't gotten up the courage to ask for a divorce until she was pregnant with their daughter, and she'd been informed by a lawyer that it could just be pregnancy hormones and the state would not allow her to get a divorce. She'd been furious and defeated all at the same time. So she'd bided her time, but then when Piper had been born, Nicholas had changed back into the man she'd known before their vows. So she'd given him the benefit of the doubt. By the time she'd realized her mistake, she had no way to fend for herself and a divorce wasn't possible.

"Why are you offering my friends and me a place to stay? You don't know us. Or do you always go around offering strange women a place to stay in your castle?" she asked.

His lips tipped up on the corner. "You're nae just any woman, lass."

"Jess," she said.

He glanced her way.

"It's my name. Jessalyn Delaney."

"It's a pleasure to meet you, Jessalyn. I'm sorry about the circumstances, though."

"It's not your fault I married an abusive asshole. If anyone is to blame, it's me."

He reached over and took her hand. "Lass, it's nae your fault. Your ex is to blame, and only him. He had the choice to be a good man or nae, and he chose nae to be one. Every man has inside of him the possibility of being bad, but most would ne'er dream of harmin' a woman. I know I wouldnae."

She gave his hand a gentle squeeze. "Then you're a good man, Tavish MacBride. There aren't as many of you out there as you seem to think. If there were, there wouldn't be a need for women's shelters."

"True enough, I suppose. "

When they reached the castle, Jess's jaw dropped. When he'd said castle, she hadn't really been expecting a *castle*. The only ones she'd heard about in the area were historical sites or ruins. The building in front of her looked like it had been around for hundreds of years, each stone lovingly placed by hand to erect the impressive structure before her. Tavish punched in the code at the iron gate, and then they pulled down the long drive and stopped by the front door.

She got out when Tavish did, accepting the arm

around her waist as he led her up to the front door. Jess stepped inside, and her breath caught in her throat at the beauty of the place. A sense of rightness filled her, as if she belonged there. The building seemed to welcome her. For the first time in her life, she felt like she was exactly where she was supposed to be. She knew it sounded insane, but she couldn't shake the feeling.

"Tavish," a woman's voice called out. A woman who didn't look a day over fifty stepped into the front entry. "I didnae realize we had company."

Tavish's arm tightened around her waist. "Mother, this is Jessalyn Delaney. She and her friends will be stayin' with us for a little while."

His mother perused her from her head to her toes, then back again, her gaze resting on the bruise on Jess's cheek. "And does that mark have anythin' to do with it?"

"Aye, a bit. I promised her she would be safe here."

"Tavish, I've raised you, dinnae lie to me now. There's more going on than you're sayin'."

A low growl came from Tavish and Jess tensed, waiting to see what he would do. How a man treated his mother told Jess a lot, which was why she should have stayed away from Nicholas when she'd realized he loathed his mother. He'd given her the excuse that his mother had a bad drug habit, but she had to wonder how much of that was true.

"We'll discuss it later, Mother. Right now, I'd like to get Jess settled into her room."

"The yellow room, I think," his mother said.

"No."

His mother's eyebrows went up. "Then where do you plan to place the girl and her friends if nae on the hall for guests?"

"She'll go in the green bear room."

His mother's eyes widened, and she paled a bit as her gaze flicked back to Jess then back to her son. "Are you sure, Tavish?"

"I'm positive, Mother."

The woman visibly swallowed and nodded, moving out of their way. "Let me know if you need anything. I'll be sewing in the front parlor."

Without another word, the woman disappeared. Tavish's words had Jess puzzled, though. Why wouldn't she be placed in the same hall as her friends? And where was this green bear room he spoke of? His mother had seemed shocked he would put Jess there. Was it reserved for special guests?

The man guiding her through the halls of his home was a mystery in more ways than one. Sometimes, when he spoke, it was almost like he was talking in code. While she had been part of the conversation with his mother, Jess had felt very much like she wasn't. Everything they'd said had been in English, but she hadn't understood a word of it. Was there more to this mountain of a man than Jess had first realized? Would she come to regret staying with him? She hoped not. She couldn't handle too many more surprises in her life.

Chapter Three

After Tavish had shown Jess to her room, he'd stepped out onto the back veranda to breathe in the crisp, clean air and try to get his mate's scent out of his head. If he'd stayed near her much longer, he would have made a fool of himself for sure. Just one whiff and he'd needed to find out more about her. Now that he'd breathed her in a while longer, he knew who she was to him, and that he wanted her above all others. And now she was staying in his home. It was where she was supposed to be, but he didn't like having her in a different room. He'd fought every instinct when he'd taken her upstairs, his bear urging him to put her in their room. Both beast and man alike wanted to see that beautiful hair spread across the pillows on their bed.

His mother came up beside him. "Are you sure?"

He cast her a glance before looking back out over his land. "Aye, I'm sure. She's the one."

"But she's… human."

"You've ne'er had a problem with me datin' a human before," he pointed out.

"Maybe not, but this one is different, Tavish. She's been abused. What makes you think she's strong enough to be the alpha's mate?"

"Because she's destined to be mine, Mother. The gods wouldnae have chosen a weak woman for me. I dinnae ken why she stayed with such an abusive man for so long, but I'm sure she had her reasons, and when she's comfortable enough she'll share them."

"Plenty of bears mate someone other than their true mate," his mother said.

He growled low, making her take a hasty step back.

"There are plenty of sows," she began, but he cut her off.

"I'll nae bed a woman other than my true mate. Now that I've found her, I'm nae letting go. Father may have married you, Mother, but we both know the two of you were miserable your entire married lives. Do you really wish that for me? A life of regret and want? Because that's what I'd have without Jess."

His mother's shoulders slumped, and she nodded her head. "Verra well, Tavish. If the lass is what you want, she's what you'll have. I will nae stand in your way."

"I love you, Mother, but I ken this is the best path for me, the *right* path. She's what I've been wanting, what I've been needin' all these years, and now that she's here I'm nae lettin' go. I'll do whate'er I have to for her to stay by my side."

"As you wish, Tavish. I only hope it disnae blow up in your face. A woman like that is goin' to require special treatment. You cannae just toss her to the bed and lift her skirts like you would any other lass. She's bound to be skittish."

"I'll keep it in mind." His lips twitched. The fact that his mother was warning him to be careful with Jess told him that she cared more than she let on. She might pretend to prefer he mate a sow, but in the end, he knew she was secretly thrilled he'd chosen his true mate over someone more convenient even if it would be a hard road to travel.

"What are you goin' to do with the lass for now? You put her in the chamber next to yours. You cannae mean to mate her so soon."

He shrugged. "If I thought she'd accept my bear so soon, I'd mate her now. It would give me e'en more reason to protect her. The town kens our unusual ability to shift, they know the term 'mate', and would ken she was more precious to me than anyone else."

"Baby steps, Tavish. Don't scare the poor thing off."

"Aye, Mother." He gave her a quick hug. "I'm goin' for a quick run. Calder, Quinn, and Gavan will return shortly with her friends and all their belongings. Put them in the guest quarters."

"Verra well. I'll play hostess until you return, or until your mate is up to the task of takin' o'er the duties of runnin' the castle."

Tavish kissed his mother's cool cheek. "I'm sure Jess will need your help and support, Mother. She's nae goin' to run you off."

His mother huffed and held out her hands, waiting for his clothes. Tavish stripped quickly and handed the bundle of clothing to his mother before letting the shift overtake him. His bones cracked and realigned, pushing him to all fours as fur sprouted over his body, pushing through his skin. His fingers curled into toes with sharp claws. As his change finished, he let out a roar before bounding across the open meadow toward the tree line.

A scent teased his nose as he cleared the steps and he almost turned. Convincing himself he was just imagining his mate's scent, he bounded forward, his paws digging into the soft grass as he neared the sanctuary of the trees. If he stayed near the castle, he knew he would want to go to *her*. He'd never felt such an intense pull to anyone before and he wasn't sure how long he could ignore it. His bear was rather insistent that they make Jess theirs, claiming her in all ways.

Rubbing his back against a tree, he scent marked his territory. He sharpened his claws on a few trees, before running toward the small loch on his property. If he were smart he'd always run here, but he missed the freedom of being in the wild. Walls closed the property in, making him feel caged even on the hundreds of acres they owned.

He splashed along the banks, enjoying his freedom, until he heard a twig snap. His ears twitched as his head turned toward the direction of the sound. A soft breeze blew and his nose twitched, denying what his senses were telling him. No way was his mate out here. She was safely tucked into bed at the castle, where he'd left her. Wasn't she? He left the water and ambled along the shore, looking toward the trees, trying to see her. When she stepped out into the open, his heart kicked in his chest. She looked both fearful and awed.

Slowly, he moved toward her, ready to stop if she looked ready to bolt.

"Y-you're a bear," she said softly, almost too softly for him to hear it. A shaky hand reached toward him, then jerked back. He didn't want her to fear him, but he wasn't sure what to do.

Jess edged closer and he could hear her heart racing, scent her fear and confusion. Tavish wanted to assure her he would never harm her, but he worried that shifting in front of her might make matters worse. How much had she seen or heard at the castle? How had she followed him without him being any the wiser?

She came a little closer still, reaching for him again. Tavish lowered his massive head, sitting and waiting to see what she would do. When her fingers skimmed through his fur between his ears, he let out a rumble of pleasure. It caused her to yank her hand away and jump back a step so he lay down, trying to look as helpless and safe as a fifteen-hundred-pound grizzly could.

When she came close again, he rubbed his head against her, scenting her. He wanted her to smell like him, for everyone to know that she belonged to him. That she allowed it made his heart warm. Maybe there was hope for them. Maybe she wouldn't run in terror if he shifted back right now. He needed to know how much she knew.

He felt the magick begin to swirl through him as the shift began.

* * *

Jess hadn't been able to help overhearing Tavish's conversation with his mother, and when he'd spoken of bears and shifting, she'd thought he was crazy. She knew of other shapeshifters -- her ex had been one after all -- but bears? She felt like she'd fallen into the pages of a storybook.

When she'd followed him, had watched him splashing in the loch, her curiosity had outweighed her fear and she'd been unable to stay away from him. She felt a pull toward him, as if she were supposed to be here right now, sharing this moment with him. If what he'd told his mother was right, she was his mate -- if she'd believed in such a crazy thing. After living with Nicholas for so long, she wasn't sure she believed in mates. He'd claimed she was destined for him and look how that had turned out. Never again would she blindly trust a man.

She watched as Tavish changed from a bear to a very naked, mouthwatering man. Her gaze scanned his body, her eyes not obeying her order to remain above waist level. Seeing his rather impressive cock had her jaw dropping a bit and her gaze snapping back up to his eyes. Just in time to see a masculine smirk grace his lips.

"Like what you see, lass?" he asked.

She felt her cheeks burn with embarrassment. "You're a bear."

"Aye, I'm a bear. You dinnae seem o'erly surprised that you're in the presence of a shapeshifter."

"I lived with one for eighteen years. I did not, however, know there were were-bears. Is that the right term? Were-bear?" Her mind still spun with the knowledge.

He nodded. "Were-bear is good enough. Either I frighten you, or you're rather excited to be so near me."

A scowl graced her face. "I'm not excited to be near you. How would you react if suddenly you knew there were were-bears running around? It was one thing knowing Nicholas could kill me in his shifted form if he wanted to, but you could literally lay me out with one swipe of your paw without even trying!"

He gave a very bear-like bark of agitation. "I'll nae harm you, lass. Have I nae already claimed as much? You're safe with me, and with my family. We'll do everythin' in our power to protect you."

She arched a brow. "Because I'm your mate? Is that why I'm in the room next to yours?"

He scrubbed a hand through his hair. "Is there anythin' you didnae hear? That was a private conversation with my mother."

"Sorry." She gave a sheepish shrug. "I was making my way outside to get some fresh air when I heard the two of you talking. Since I seemed to be the topic of conversation, I couldn't stop myself from listening in."

"It's mostly because you're my mate, but I'd like to think I'd help any lass in need."

Her gaze skimmed over him again and her cheeks flushed. "Maybe you should change back into a bear. Until you have some clothes to put on."

He gave her a knowing smile and folded his arms over his broad chest, flexing for her. Jess had to admit she wasn't unaffected by the sexy Highlander, even if she did tell herself that she should keep away from him. The man had trouble written all over him, and trouble was the last thing she needed. Besides, again, it wasn't the first time a man had claimed she was his mate. Just because he said it didn't make it true. Jess had learned early on that she wasn't Nicholas's mate regardless of what he'd said. If she had been, he never would have laid a hand on her. She did know enough about shapeshifters to know they revered their mates.

"Does my lack of pants trouble you, lass?"

Her cheeks warmed even more. "You don't even know me. Doesn't it bother you to stand there completely naked?"

He arched a brow. "Does it look like I have anythin' to be ashamed of?"

She cleared her throat and looked away, but her gaze was drawn back to him. He was the flame and she was the moth, helpless against his magnetic pull. There was no way she could deny that there was sexual chemistry between them, but she'd made it this long without sex and she could last a while longer. Her future might look bleak, but at least she would have her kids and they would all be safe if she could ever get rid of Nicholas.

"All right, lass. I'll change back, but only because it makes you uncomfortable to see me this way."

Unable to watch his transformation, she turned her back, choosing instead to watch the woods surrounding her. She could hear the sound of his bones cracking and reforming and tried to contain the shiver that ran through her. While Jess had never had the ability to shift, she'd always thought it looked rather painful. A large, furry head nudged her, and she looked down. Tavish had come up beside her in his bear form.

She couldn't help but smile. He made a beautiful bear, even if her heart did race a little at his nearness. She wasn't sure if it was from the excitement of discovering bear shifters, like she'd told him, or if it was something more. Maybe it was half excitement and half desire. What woman could look at him sans clothes and not be reduced to a puddle of goo?

"Don't go spouting that mate nonsense around my friends," she warned. "I'm not falling for it a second time and getting them on your side will just piss me off. Monica may seem like a hard-ass, but she's a romantic at heart."

He snorted and nudged her with his shoulder, nearly knocking her over.

She shoved him back. "Watch it, Baloo."

He let out a low growl to show his irritation, but she glowered at him. "If you don't want me to crack bear jokes, maybe you shouldn't shove me around with your massive body."

Tavish gazed at her with those bottomless, soulful bear eyes of his and she sighed. He had to be the one animal she loved above all others. Walking beside him was probably the highlight of her life, other than being a mother. She'd never have guessed she'd get to be so close to a real live bear. Yet here she was, taking a stroll through the woods with one. All right, so he was really a man-bear, but she wouldn't be picky.

Truthfully, if there were going to be a Mr. Perfect

for her, she couldn't think of anyone more adequate for the job than Tavish. He was chivalrous, sexy as hell, and transformed into her favorite animal. And that Scot's accent! Lord but she could listen to the man talk for hours. Not that she would admit to any of that. Not even to Monica, and she knew her friend was going to have some questions for her, especially if she discovered they were guests of were-bears.

At the house, Tavish's clothes were folded neatly on the rail of the veranda. Jess walked up the stairs and patiently waited, with her back to him, while he dressed. She heard the sounds of him shifting back and winced at the snap, crackle, and pop. There was a rustle of clothing, then a hand landed on her shoulder.

"I think we should talk, lass," Tavish said, turning her to face him. "You mentioned your Nicholas was a shifter. That changes things a bit."

"How?"

He smiled. "It means we follow my rules and nae human rules. He's tryin' to harm my mate, and that I'll nae stand for. Without you, there will be no future chief of the MacBride clan. You're essential to my clan and I'm sure the local police would see it my way. They'll nae stand by while he tries to harm you."

"I thought you wanted to do things the shifter way. Why involve the police?"

His smile broadened. "Lass, our police *are* shifters. Nae bears like the MacBrides, but most of the police are Murdochs."

"And Murdochs are what exactly?"

"Wolves."

"Lions and tigers and bears, oh my," she mumbled.

"You've nae fallen into Oz. Now, tell me what type of shifter your ex-husband is so we can begin to formulate a plan of attack."

"Coyote."

His eyebrows arched. "You shackled yourself to the likes of a coyote? And you're still here to tell the tale? Coyotes are a nasty lot, lass. I'm nae surprised he harmed you." His expression turned fierce. "Did he harm the wee ones too?"

She looked away a moment. "He would drag them down the hall to their rooms by their hair, then whip them, sometimes with a belt or a riding crop. He liked to call my daughter names. Telling her she was stupid or lazy, sometimes calling her a bitch."

Tavish mumbled something under his breath that she couldn't quite catch, but it sounded like he was cussing.

"It's in the past, Tavish. I appreciate your concern, but Nicholas couldn't care less about the kids. It's me he likes to torment. I think if I hadn't shown any sign that his treatment of them bothered me, he probably would have left them alone. At least he never hurt them when they were babies."

Thunder boomed and Jess jumped. She felt the blood drain from her face and her knees knocked together.

"Scared of storms?" Tavish asked.

"Something like that."

He took her hand in his, giving it a gentle squeeze. "Then let's get you inside before the rain starts."

Chapter Four

Tavish ignored the chatter at the dinner table as he focused on his mate. Jess was still deathly pale, flinching every time it thundered. He'd be willing to bet her ex had something to do with her reaction to the storm raging outside, but he wasn't sure how to get her to open up, to learn to trust him. He'd give his life for her, but she didn't seem willing to believe she was his mate. He couldn't really blame her, not after her ex-husband had lied to her and abused her and her children. It still baffled him that a man could harm his own cubs.

Her friends seemed to be getting along well with his brothers, and Tavish wondered if there might be a budding romance or two there. None of his brothers had mentioned finding their mates amongst the group of women, but that didn't mean they couldn't have a bit of pleasure while the lasses were around. Then again, his mate might not take too kindly to his brothers playing with her friends. Maybe he should warn them away.

Another clap of thunder rattled the windows and Jess's hand shook as she lifted her fork to her mouth. He reached over and placed a comforting hand on top of hers, hoping to ease her fears. He'd pull her into his arms if he thought she'd allow it. Tavish figured she would fight him like a wild cat if he were to try coddling her. It was doubtful she'd been shown much kindness since her marriage to the other shifter, but that was one thing he planned to change as quickly as possible.

An idea began to form. What if he showed her he was truly her mate, that her well-being was everything to him? If he proved he cared, say, enough to bring her children to Scotland, wouldn't that prove that he wanted more from her than a fling? Although, he had a feeling a fling would be easier for her to accept than a true mating. He had his work cut out for him.

The meal came to an end, and while he wanted to go to Jess, he pulled Monica aside instead.

The woman arched her brows at him. "What? Your charm not working on her so you thought you'd switch to me?"

"Nae hardly. Jess is mine, whether she wants to admit it or nae. No, what I need from you is a wee bit of help. I'd like to bring her children here, but I dinnae ken how to contact their guardians."

Monica pursed her lips. "They're staying with their grandparents, Jess's parents. As far as I know, the kids have passports from a trip they went on with the grandparents last summer. But why should her family believe you truly want them here? How do they know you won't harm them just like their father has?"

Tavish scowled at her. "Dinnae e'er compare me to that bawbag."

"Why should I believe you're any different than him? You're both animals. Don't deny it. Jessalyn tells me everything. She's my best friend."

He snarled, baring his teeth. "I'm nae an animal. I'm a shapeshifter, a bear, and alpha of my kind, nae to mention chief of my clan. My position demands honor and respect, but I dinnae get it by being a bully to those who are weaker than me. Ask anyone in my clan and they'll tell you I'm a fair man."

"Fine. Let's say I do help you. What makes you think bringing the kids here is such a great idea? Shouldn't you contain their father before bringing them to the castle?"

"Can you think of anywhere safer than the castle

grounds? He cannae enter the gates, and if they wish to see the village, I'll make sure to escort them myself or assign two of my brothers to them. They will nae be unprotected while on MacBride lands."

Monica looked confused. "You sound almost possessive of them, like they're yours or something."

"They are mine. They are the children of my mate, which makes them my cubs, e'en if they arenae mine by blood. I will raise them as my own and treat them accordingly."

Monica's expression went from skeptical to slightly disbelieving. "You honestly expect me to believe you're going to love them, sight unseen? What if they drive you crazy? What if they hate you on sight?"

"Then we'll work through those things. They're important to my mate. Therefore, they are important to me. Children are to be loved and cherished, nae treated like they dinnae matter."

"You're saying everything right, Tavish MacBride. I guess we'll see if you follow through. I'll give you their grandparents' number, but when this blows up in your face I'll be the first one to say 'I told you so.'"

"It wilnae come to that, I assure you. Just think how happy Jess will be to see her kids."

"Or maybe she's happy to be away from them for the first time in a year. Did you ever think that this was her vacation? It's the first time she's been single and without kids in eighteen years. She's devoted her life to her family, and it's time for her to relax for a while."

Tavish frowned. "I admit, I dinnae know her verra well, but I have a hard time picturin' Jess being upset over seeing her children. She seems like the motherly type to me."

"Fine. We'll do it your way." Monica pulled her cell phone out of her pocket. "Do you want the number now?"

"Aye, now will be fine."

She rattled off the number, and Tavish programmed it into his phone. He'd wait and call when he knew he would be alone for a while. He wasn't sure how to approach his future in-laws, since they'd never met him. Would they react to his mate claim the same way Jess had? With reservations and skepticism? He hoped that bringing her kids here would break down some of the walls Jess had erected.

He searched the castle for Jess, finally coming to the realization that she must have gone to her room. He knocked and didn't hear an answer. Remembering her unease earlier, he tried to quietly turn the knob, needing to assure himself she was safe. Just as he stepped inside, thunder boomed, and the lights flickered out. Jess screamed and he hurried to her side, pulling her off the bed and into his arms.

"It's just the storm, lass. Nothin' here will hurt you," he assured her. Her body shook as she clutched at his shirt.

"You must think I'm silly," she said, her voice muffled as she buried her face against him.

"No, lass. I dinnae think you're silly. Do you want to talk about it?"

She slowly lifted her head. "Do you really want to hear about my life with Nicholas? It isn't a pretty story."

"Only what you want to tell me. I'll nae push you for more." Not at the moment, he amended. Sooner or later, he would get the entire story from her. But right now, she needed comfort and maybe someone to talk to. It was obvious her life with her ex-husband had affected her, and still did. He could only imagine what she'd been through, her and the kids.

She looked around. "We should probably sit."

He eyed the lone chair by the window, then the bed. No, if they sat on the bed, he'd want to do other things, and Tavish didn't think she was ready for that yet. He hoped she would be someday soon because he wanted to mark her as his, to claim her for all the world to see.

"I have more places to sit in my room," he offered.

She looked hesitant for a moment, but nodded her consent. He took her by the hand and led her next door. She didn't seem surprised she was next to his room, but then she'd listened to most of his conversation with his mother. Little did she realize that she was in the room reserved for the lady of the castle. A room no one had slept in since his parents were first courting.

As he stepped into his room, he let go of her hand long enough to light a few candles. The power going out was a common enough occurrence that he was prepared for the occasion.

Jess shied away from the chairs by the window and instead claimed a seat by the fireplace. Tavish motioned toward it.

"Would you like a fire, lass?"

"It's a bit chilly in here," she said as a shiver raked her.

Tavish knelt and began placing wood in the grate before adding kindling and setting a match to it. When the fire caught and the logs blazed to life, he blew out the match and claimed the seat next to Jess. As thunder rattled the windows, he watched her grip the arms of her chair until her knuckles turned white. He had to do something to take her mind off the storm and lack of power.

"How did you meet Nicholas?" he asked.

"Someone at work introduced us at a party. He was charming and seemed sweet, always had a smile for me. I fell head over heels for him almost instantly. Then I learned he was a shapeshifter, quite by accident, and he told me about mates and that the two of us were destined to be together."

"And you believed him?"

She shrugged. "I'd seen him change with my own eyes, and I'd read enough paranormal romances to understand the basics as far as mates went. So when he declared I was his, I thought all my dreams were coming true."

Tavish frowned. "When did you find out all wasnae as it seemed?"

"Our wedding night. He barked orders at me, sneered if I didn't move fast enough, and when it came time to consummate our marriage he was… rough. From that night on, I seldom saw him smile, unless it was a cruel one. He delighted in tormenting me, making me hurt both physically and emotionally. I had to quit my job because I couldn't always hide the bruises, and they would only buy that whole 'I ran into a door' story so many times."

"The way you speak of your ex, he seems to the sort to make you quit."

"Not that time. A few years later I tried to get another job, just waiting tables to have a little extra spending money. We had the kids by then and I wanted to be able to take them places. Nicholas found out and became livid. He beat me that night, badly enough that I needed a hospital, and swore that it was only the beginning if I didn't quit my job. I didn't realize it right then, but later it occurred to me that he wanted me weak and helpless, dependent on him."

"Hurdie," Tavish mumbled under his breath.

"Pardon?" Jess's brow puckered.

"I said he's an arsehole."

That term she understood, if the smile on her face was anything to go by. He was certain she'd called him that several times herself, especially since being free of the man. He'd have to watch his language once the kids arrived, assuming he could convince their grandparents to send them to Scotland. The grandparents would be welcome too, if they wanted to come. It wasn't like he didn't have space for everyone.

"Anyway, he left the kids alone until they reached about six years old. He'd only yell at them before that. It was like he felt they were big enough to take the beating he gave them. I can't understand anyone wanting to harm their own children."

"Do they shift?" Tavish asked.

"They can," Jess said, "but they don't. I think they're too scared that it will make them like their father. It's sad because they're beautiful in their animal forms."

"So they turn into coyotes like your ex."

"Actually, Nicholas's entire family isn't made up of coyotes. He took after his father, but when he watched Piper shift the first time, he confessed that his mother hadn't been a coyote, but another type of shapeshifter."

Tavish folded his arms and waited patiently.

"She was, um, a platypus."

Tavish nearly strangled on the laugh he was trying to hold back. It wouldn't do to laugh at his future daughter's other form. Although, he'd bet it was cute on a girl. A man, not so much.

"And Donovan?" he asked.

"Coyote. I think he's the most scared to shift, worried that he'll take after his dad in other ways."

Tavish shook his head. "Denyin' what he is wilnae change things. If anythin', a lack of shifting could make things worse. He'll become irritable when his animal wants out to run, and if he goes long enough without shifting, he could become violent as he gets older. By denyin' himself, he's on the path to becomin' the type of man he disnae want to turn into."

Jess licked her lips. "I wish he could meet you, get a chance to talk to your brothers and you, see how shifters are supposed to live. Maybe if he were around strong men, men who didn't use that strength to intimidate and harm women, then he would learn to be the kind of man he wants to be."

Tavish smiled. "I had planned to surprise you, but would you be all right with the kids comin' here for a visit?"

"I could barely afford this trip just for me. If my parents and Monica hadn't helped, I wouldn't have been able to come." She shook her head. "There's no way I could bring the kids here."

Tavish waved away her concerns. "Those are my future children, once you accept you're my mate. Let me worry about gettin' them here."

She pursed her lips. "Are you still going on about me being your mate? Because I don't believe it. If I were your mate, if it was anything like I read in my books, then…"

"Then what, lass?" he asked with an arched brow.

Her cheeks bloomed with color. "Then you wouldn't be able to keep your hands off me."

"Lass, you have no idea how temptin' you are.

Just because I'm nae givin' in to my baser urges disnae mean I dinnae want you. My bear has been a noisy bastard, wantin' to mark you and claim you as ours."

She paled. "Mark?"

He reached over and smoothed her hair back from her face. "Nae the kind of marks Nicholas left on you. This is a bite that will go on your shoulder. It's how all shifters mark their mates."

"Nicholas didn't do that," she said.

"It only goes to prove that you were nae truly his mate. If you were, he'd have marked you. There's no way he'd have lasted eighteen years without properly claimin' you. He lied to you so you would fall in line with his plans. Maybe he thought you were weak and he could intimidate you. I dinnae know why he chose you, lass, and only he can truly answer that question. I do ken that he was wrong. You're strong, Jess, so verra strong. You had to be to survive livin' with him, to have the courage to break free."

"A strong woman, a *smart* woman, would have never fallen for his lies."

He cupped her cheek. "Dinnae think badly of yourself for fallin' for his tricks. It could have happened to anyone. If I had to guess, I'd say you were lookin' for love and didnae question it when it came along. You had stars in your eyes, and there's nothin' wrong with that, lass."

"Thank you," she said softly. "If you want to bring the children here, I won't object. If you'd like, I can mention it to my parents."

"I had planned to call them a little later tonight, or tomorrow afternoon."

"Then we can call them together. They don't know you, so they won't entrust the kids to you. But if I explain things…"

"That I'm a shifter and you're my mate?"

She nibbled on her lower lip. "I don't know if I should mention that part."

Tavish smiled. "You tell them whate'er you need to, lass. Just know that I will welcome the children into my home as if they were my verra own. Your cubs are my cubs." His smile broadened. "Although, I have thought a time or two since seein' you about havin' cubs with you of my own."

She blushed a becoming shade of pink. "I think it's a little early for that."

He nodded. "Maybe. You'll let me know when you're ready. Until then, I can be a verra patient man. Knowin' you're under my roof will have to appease the beast for a while."

She held out her hand. "May I borrow your phone? We might as well get this call out of the way. Besides, it will keep my mind off the storm."

Tavish pulled out his phone and handed it to her. As she called her parents, he studied her in the firelight, admiring her striking features. Some might call her girl-next-door pretty, but to him she was the most gorgeous woman he'd ever seen, and his bear was in complete agreement. They were lucky bastards to have been tied to such a creature as Jess. If she would only agree to the mating, then everything would be damn near perfect -- once he got rid of Nicholas, something he planned to work on first thing in the morning. He'd get the police involved if he had to, but he hoped he could resolve the problem shifter style. There wasn't a more important task than protecting your mate and cubs. Tavish would attack the job with gusto, anxious to ease his mate's mind.

As she handed him the phone, he prepared himself for the awkward questions his future in-laws were sure to have. But he would go through anything for Jess, no matter how uncomfortable it made him. She was worth it.

Chapter Five

The next morning, Tavish took a quick shower before donning a white button-down shirt and his plaid. If he was going to tackle the problem of Nicholas, he wanted to look every inch the Highland Chief that he was. Besides, a plaid was quicker to get out of than a pair of jeans if the need to shift arose. He hoped it didn't come to that, but he'd take whatever measures were necessary to protect his mate and cubs.

As he stepped out of his room, a disheveled Jess came out of hers. Gods, but she looked delectable first thing in the morning with her hair hanging to her waist in a half-brushed state, her clothes looking both comfortable and sexy with her top hanging off one shoulder. He wanted to place his lips against the skin there and flick his tongue along the silky expanse.

"Morning," she said, rubbing sleep from her eyes.

"You're up awfully early, lass. It's barely seven."

She shrugged a shoulder. "I'm used to getting up early to help the kids get ready for school. No matter where I am, once the sun starts coming through my windows I'm awake. I can't seem to shut it off even when they aren't here."

"I haednae planned to stay for breakfast this morn, but if you'd like a bit of company I could change my plans."

"Where are you off to so early?" she asked as they headed toward the stairs.

"I have a wee bit of business to attend to this mornin'."

She glanced at him from the corner of her eye. "The kind that involves Nicholas?"

"Maybe."

She stopped and placed a hand on his arm. "Be careful, Tavish. Nicholas doesn't play fair. Once he realizes you're after him, he'll do anything to stay one step ahead of you. And if he thinks for one moment the two of us are together, he'll stop at nothing to destroy the both of us. He thinks I belong to him, even though we're divorced. I've felt like he was stalking me, even before this trip, but I never had proof."

They continued down the stairs and he mulled over her words.

"Stalkin' you how, lass?"

"I'd get phone calls at all hours from an unlisted number, but there wasn't a way for me to track it and if I called it back there would be no answer and no voicemail set up. I can't prove it was Nicholas calling me, but I *feel* like it was him. There were other times when I felt like I was being followed. And then there was the time..." She trailed off.

"The time what?"

"The time I went out to take the kids to school and all four of my tires had been slashed during the night. The police said it was just pranksters in the neighborhood, but I've never had trouble from the local kids. I just know it was Nicholas, even though I didn't have any evidence against him."

"You should always trust your instincts, Jess. If you believe it was him, then it was. No one kens him better than you. But I hope to put a stop to all of it once and for all. He can either go home on his own, or he can have a wee bit of help gettin' there."

"Just don't get into trouble."

Tavish smiled. "They'll nae arrest me for defending my family, lass. Ne'er fear."

"I just don't want something bad to happen to you," she admitted as they entered the kitchen. She worried at her lower lip and Tavish reached out to smooth it before she made herself bleed.

"Nothin' will happen to me, *mo ghradh*." Before she could ask him what the endearment meant, he swiftly introduced her to Rhona and Cook before ordering their breakfast. Why he'd slipped and said such a thing, he wasn't sure, but he'd have to make sure it didn't happen again.

Instead of moving to the dining room, Jess made herself comfortable at the scarred kitchen table and Tavish claimed the seat next to her. It wasn't the first time he'd enjoyed a cup of coffee with his staff, but they still gave him quizzical looks. So what if he wanted to enjoy a peaceful morning with his mate? If she wanted to sit in the kitchen, that's where they would sit.

They tucked into the breakfast and Tavish waited to see if she'd have any other concerns or questions for him. Quite honestly, he wasn't sure what to say to her. They were still very much strangers, even if they were destined to spend their lives together. He looked forward to getting to know her better, in all ways, but he wasn't sure how to go about it. He'd always been a ladies' man but with his mate, he was at a loss as to how to act. She wasn't just *any* woman, she was *his* woman, and that made all the difference in the world.

Cook and Rhona stepped out to give them a little privacy, each casting a glance at Tavish that clearly said *Don't screw this up*. He knew they wouldn't be gone long, but maybe he could get his mate to talk to him before they returned. Learn more about her.

"You never said what your brothers and you do for a living," Jess said between bites. "I would imagine a place like this costs a lot to keep up."

"My family has always invested well, so we

dinnae have to work if we dinnae want to. I tend to play the stock market. Gavan likes to work with his hands and makes furniture that he sells in local shops. Quinn owns a security company. And Calder… well, Calder is still figurin' out what to do with his life. As the baby of the family he's been coddled, perhaps a wee bit too much." He took a swallow of his coffee. "And what is it you do, Jess?"

"I took the easy way out and moved in with my sister while I looked for another job. It's been six months since I left Nicholas, but jobs aren't easy to come by, especially when you've been out of work for so long. I've found a few temp jobs, but they only last a few days to a week. I'm competing against college graduates who are fresh out of school and can work for less money than me."

"If you could do anythin', what would it be?"

She smiled. "I'd like to work in a library. I love books, of all kinds, and being around them day in and out sounds rather peaceful. Not to mention how fulfilling it would be to help others on the quest for finding the perfect book."

"Would you now?" He smiled. "It just so happens that our wee library was recently expanded and is lookin' for a bit of help."

She tilted her head. "You do realize this is just a vacation for me, right? I'm going home in a week."

He couldn't quite stifle the growl that rumbled out of him at the thought of his mate leaving. "I thought we covered that last night. You're meant to be here, with me. I dinnae plan for you to return to your country, as this is your home now."

Her eyebrows arched and he realized that perhaps he shouldn't have sounded so… caveman-like. It was the shifter in him and it couldn't be helped, but he would definitely have to watch his words in the future.

"I didnae mean it like that, lass. But as my mate, your place is here by my side. Surely you ken that."

"What I understand is that you *think* I'm your mate. Just because you declare it so doesn't mean I have to dump everything I've been working for and move my children and my belongings how many miles away? They have a home there. Family. We may be struggling, but we've been trying to start over. I don't want to uproot them even more just because you've decided we're destined to be together."

"What's it goin' to take, lass? What can I do to make you realize how important you are to me? There has to be somethin', some way for me to prove what I tell you is true, that I'm nae lying to you like your Nicholas did."

"I don't know." She stared into her cup. "Maybe... maybe once Nicholas is firmly in my past, I can think about the future, but right now it's about surviving. It would be so easy to go along with you, Tavish, to just hand my life over to you and follow your lead, but I did that once before with Nicholas and look what it got me."

He took her hand in his. "Lass, I'd ne'er ask you to hand your life o'er to me. I want us to face each day together with you by my side, nae standin' in my shadow."

She looked like she wanted to believe him, and he hoped she'd be able to. If he got his hands on Nicholas, he'd likely strangle the man. He hadn't just crushed Jess's spirit, he'd crushed her dreams and taken away all her hope. He'd destroyed her in every way a man could destroy a woman, and for that he would pay -- dearly.

"I can't promise you forever, Tavish, but I'm willing to give you a chance. That's the best I can do right now. I'll call the airline and let them know I won't be returning when I'd planned. I won't schedule another flight just yet, but… I'm not agreeing to stay here forever."

"All I ask for is time, lass. Time to prove you're meant to be mine."

Rhona bustled back through the door, no doubt having been listening on the other side. She started cleaning the kitchen, not looking at either of them, but he knew she was aware of everything going on. She never missed anything.

After breakfast he made sure Jess had everything she needed, and then he left for his reckoning with Nicholas. So the man liked to talk with his fists when it came to women? Tavish wanted to see just how brave the coyote would be when faced with a man instead. Tavish had no doubt he could crush the other shifter if it came down to it, but maybe he could make the man see reason. He had three days until his cubs arrived from the States and he wanted the problem taken care of before then. He'd convinced Jess to cancel her return flight home, not permanently, but just long enough to give them some more time together, and to give the kids a chance to enjoy Scotland. He couldn't wait to take them to the loch to shift.

Quinn stood in the front entry, ready and waiting. He followed Tavish outside. Tavish's skin twitched with the urge to shift. He wanted to confront the coyote in his bear form, but Tavish wasn't sure that was the best decision. If the need arose, he'd take Nicholas out any way necessary, but first he'd attempt to be civil. Somewhat.

"You sure this is wise?" Quinn asked. "He's the

father of her cubs."

"Aye, he is. He's also one to use his fists on her and those cubs. She wilnae miss him when he's gone. She wants peace, Quinn. I'll do whate'er it takes to give it to her." He shoved his hands in his pockets. "He convinced her she was his mate. He's broken her trust nae just in him, but in all men. She's scared, Quinn. I dinnae just see the fear in her eyes, I can smell it. No woman should ever be afraid for her life or that of her cubs because she trusted the wrong man."

Quinn nodded. "Sounds like takin' out this Nicholas would be doin' the world a favor."

"Let's find the bawbag. I want this done before the cubs arrive."

They climbed into Tavish's truck and headed toward the Sheep's Heid Inn. One way or another, they'd track Nicholas down and settle the issue once and for all. No one threatened his mate and cubs without paying the price.

The innkeeper greeted them with a smile. "Mornin'! Are the Americans settlin' in at the castle?"

Tavish nodded. "Aye. But I'm lookin' for one in particular. Goes by the name Nicholas. Is he stayin' here?"

The man's face twisted into a grimace. "He was. Asked him to leave. Too much trouble."

"What did he do?" Quinn asked.

The innkeeper's face darkened and started to reshape into that of his beast before he managed to gain control of himself. "Cornered my granddaughter in the hall."

Fury burned through him. "Is she all right?"

The man nodded. "Aye. Well enough. A bit bruised."

"We'll see her avenged," Tavish promised.

He felt his muscles swell as his bear tried to break free. His vision shifted and the scents around him became stronger. The stench of coyote was hard to miss. Tavish left the vehicle in front of the inn and followed the trail. Nicholas had cut through town and then into the woods not far from the castle. When Tavish realized he'd scaled the fence, he knew he wouldn't be holding his bear back. Not when his mate was in danger.

His bear ripped free and Tavish let out an outraged roar. His brother shifted beside him and together they knocked down the fence panel. His paws dug into the earth as he raced toward the castle, hoping he made it there before the coyote could hurt Jess.

A red haze settled over his vision as he focused on protecting what was his. No one would take Jess from him, especially a mangy coyote.

Chapter Six

Jess stared at the table after Tavish left. As much as she wanted to trust him, there was still a part of her that was too scared to trust in any man. Rhona slid a steaming cup in front of her, bringing her out of her musings. She smiled her thanks and took a sip, surprised at the taste of peppermint.

"Those boys might have a bit of a wild streak," Rhona said, "but you'll nae find a more faithful lot. If Tavish says you're his mate, he means it. It's nae the sort of thing a shifter takes lightly."

Jess wasn't sure how much to confide in the woman. If it were just her, then mating him wouldn't be quite so scary. But Jess had to think about Donovan and Piper too. Had Tavish told anyone about her kids? Or that they shifted too? His brothers knew about Nicholas. She'd assumed he'd tell others at the castle.

"My children are shifters, and so is their dad," Jess said. "I already fell for the destined mate line once. I'm not exactly eager to travel that road again. I barely survived last time."

Rhona reached over and patted her hand. "Lass, I can see you've had a hard time of it. Let Tavish show you what it means to truly be a shifter. He's the alpha, and while he may turn into a massive bear he's the gentlest soul I've ever met. I ken you're scared, as you should be. Just don't let fear blind you to the happiness you could have with him. You're meant to be together."

She took another sip of tea. "I know not all men are evil. Deep down I really do know it. Nicholas just did a number on me. He wasn't just physically abusive, but he used my children against me, made sure I had no means to support myself and had no choice but to remain with him."

"A bruised heart is often the last to heal, even long after visible marks on a body." Rhona smiled. "But listen well. Sometimes we need to trust in others, accept their help, and even their love, in order to fully mend."

"You're a wise woman, Rhona."

She patted her hand again. "You remember that. Give the lad a chance. If you let him, he'll love you fiercely and protect you always. Nae just you, but the cubs too. When Tavish loves, he does so with his whole heart."

Jess thought about her words, and what she'd experienced so far with Tavish. He'd been kind. Considerate. She couldn't deny there was a spark between them. Was her past experience holding her back from a once in a lifetime chance at love? She'd divorced Nicholas so she could live her life without fear, but she hadn't stopped to consider that living without love wasn't really living at all. If Tavish was right about destined mates, and that she belonged with him, what would she be giving up if she walked away? Not just for her, but for her kids too.

"He wants to bring the children here," she said. "They need a good example in their lives. Someone to show them the way a man should act with his family."

"Tavish would be a fine example for them to follow. But dinnae take my word for it. Let the cubs meet him and see for yourself. He will love them as if they were his own flesh and blood." Rhona paused, her head cocking and her gaze intense.

"What is it?"

She shushed Jess and turned to look at the kitchen window. With slow, silent steps, Rhona moved across the floor and peered through the glass. Jess didn't know what Rhona had thought she heard, but she hadn't noticed anything out of the ordinary. Then again, for all Jess knew, Rhona was a shifter too. Maybe her hearing was more sensitive.

She sniffed at the air and her eyes went wide as she spun to face Jess. "Run, lass! Run!"

Startled, Jess stood so fast the chair toppled to the floor. She hadn't even cleared the doorway before the kitchen window shattered and something furry snapped and snarled. The creature she knew was her ex-husband knocked Rhona to the floor, her head cracking the edge of the counter on her way down. She lay so still, Jess feared he'd killed her.

With her heart hammering in her chest, she eyed the coyote and knew it was too late. Nicholas had found her. Tavish had said she'd be safe here, but he'd been wrong. She'd survived all this time, and now Nicholas would finally kill her.

Soft chatter from the stairway caught her attention, and her hands fisted at her sides. How to warn Monica and the others? Nicholas's ears flicked and he lifted his lips, showing off his sharp fangs. He launched himself at her, knocking Jess to the floor. His hot breath fanned across her face, making her gag. Sadly, it didn't smell much better when he was in human form either.

A roar in the distance made the coyote pause. He looked over his shoulder before his gaze locked on her again. "Nicholas, please. Just let me go. You won't get away with it this time. If you hurt me or kill me, they'll track you down. Leave while you can."

He snarled and saliva dripped onto her shoulder. A shiver raked Jess's spine and she knew she needed to stall longer. The next roar was much closer. Tavish was coming. If only she could stay alive long enough…

Jess heard Monica's voice just outside the kitchen.

"Don't come in," she yelled. "Nicholas is here."

He growled and raked his claws down her arm, breaking open the skin. She stifled her cry of pain and stared down the beast hovering over her. Before he could do more damage, he tensed, then spun, going back out the window. She couldn't contain the sob that welled in her throat. Monica burst through the door with their friends on her heels. She checked Jess while Rachel looked after Rhona. Ellie hovered, her hands fluttering.

"You need a doctor," Monica said.

Another roar rent the air with another following, then a yelp. Jess hoped that meant Tavish had gotten in at least one good bite. She didn't dare believe that Nicholas would no longer be a problem. As much as she wanted the misery to end, he was too determined and too crafty, and not above cheating to get what he wanted. The man was too mean to die.

Tavish's mom rushed into the kitchen. The moment she saw Jess's arm, she clucked her tongue and grabbed a clean kitchen towel. "Press tight. I'll get Tavish."

Monica helped hold the towel in place. Her friend glanced toward Rhona, and Jess noticed she hadn't moved yet. Jess hoped she would be okay. The woman had been kind. No one deserved the brutality that always resulted when Nicholas was nearby, least of all an innocent bystander. She'd been in the wrong place at the wrong time. If Nicholas had killed the woman, Jess knew Tavish would want his blood even more than he already did.

"Is she all right?" she asked.

"She's breathing. I think she's just unconscious,"

Rachel said. "Do they have 9-1-1 here? Who do we call for help?"

Jess heard a heavy tread and turned her face toward the door. Tavish stalked into the room and knelt beside her. Her cheeks turned scarlet when she got to see more than she'd bargained for. It seemed Scotsmen really didn't wear anything under their kilts. When she felt a tingle between her legs, despite the pain in her arm, she knew she wouldn't be able to hold out against him. No one had ever made feel so desperate for their touch. She shot her gaze over to Monica, but she was too busy eyeing Tavish's brother. It wasn't the first time Jess had noticed her friend's attention wandering, and she wondered if there might be a romance on the horizon.

"Rhona will heal. She's a shifter, and tougher than she looks," Tavish's mother said.

"Let me see, lass," Tavish said, reaching for the towel. He lifted it, growling when he saw the wounds.

"Tavish, there's only one way to heal her," his mother said. "You ken what you need to do."

"She needs time," he said.

"Time for what?" Jess asked.

"To be properly mated," Tavish said. "My bite will nae only bond us, but it will also give you some extra benefits. Like faster healing, and a slightly longer lifespan."

Monica held up a hand. "Hold up. You make her your mate and she gets superpowers? Jesus, Jess! What the hell are you waiting for? You get a hunky Scotsman *and* cool new abilities. Is there a downside to all this?"

Jess opened and shut her mouth a few times before sighing. There was no way she'd ever make Monica understand. Her arm throbbed.

"He got away," Tavish said, "but nae before I

took a chunk from him. He'll heal, more's the pity."

"Nae right away though," Quinn said. "He'll need to recover a few days. Unless he has the ability to recover quickly. Some shifters do."

Tavish looked over at Quinn. "Tell everyone to watch for him. I want him found. He'll nae harm my mate again. I want the hurdie handled before the cubs arrive."

"I'll see it's done," Quinn said.

Tavish lifted Jess into his arms. "Come, lass. I'll clean your wounds and we can talk. Seems we've more to discuss."

She studied him as he carried her upstairs. He didn't take her back to the room she'd slept in. Instead, he placed her on his bed. Tavish removed her shoes and brushed her hair back from her face before stepping into the adjoining bath and getting a wet cloth. He dabbed at the torn flesh on her arm, making tears prick her eyes.

"I'll heal if you bite me?" she asked.

"Aye. More than that, you'll be mine. It's a forever sort of deal, Jess. Dinnae accept my claim lightly, for there's no goin' back." He cupped her cheek. "I'll nae hurt you. Ever. Or the cubs. I would die for my family, and that includes you."

He retrieved some ointment, gauze, and tape, then started treating her wounds and wrapping her arm. It stung, and already blood stained the bandage. She wondered if she needed stitches.

"How does it work?" she asked.

"Durin' our first matin', my fangs will drop, and I'll bite into your shoulder. My saliva will enter your blood, slightly alterin' your DNA. It will bind us together until one of us dies. I'm nae sure you're up for the matin' part, Jess. Even if I try to be gentle, my beast will take o'er. I'll nae be able to hold back."

She shifted and braced herself for the pain. Slowly, she lifted her shirt over her head and tossed it to the side. Tavish's eyes darkened and flashed a honey color as he rumbled in appreciation. She worked her pants off her hips before her bear took a step closer.

"Let me," he said, his tone reverent as he reached for her. He removed her pants before helping her sit up so he could pop the clasp on her bra. Her cheeks warmed under his appraisal, but she also felt something else. A kind of empowerment. He eyed her like a starving man would a buffet, and even licked his lips. Yet his touch was hesitant as he gripped the waistband of her panties. He held her gaze as he tugged on the material, giving her time to put a halt to things.

"I'm sure, Tavish. Don't stop."

He seemed to almost grow in size and his eyes warmed to a brighter hue, his bear so close she wondered if he was about to shift. He stripped her panties off and pushed her thighs wide. Her breath caught as he leaned down, inhaling her scent. The rasp of his tongue against her folds made her nipples harden.

"Tavish!"

He gave her a fierce grin, flashing his fangs, before he lapped at her again. He worked his tongue inside her, and she wondered if he'd partially shifted. She stared down her body at the man between her legs, but didn't see a hint of fur anywhere. Although, the hands gripping her did seem to have claws instead of fingernails.

"Tavish, I..."

He growled as he flicked his tongue in and out, driving it in deeper each time. Jess gave up, squirming on the bed as pleasure rolled over her. She'd never felt anything like it before, certainly not with Nicholas. Her nipples had tightened to the point of pain and she rubbed her fingers over them, whimpering at the light touch.

Tavish grew still between her legs and she opened her eyes, not even realizing she'd shut them. He was watching her, or more specifically, he watched her hands. She pinched her nipples and felt him shudder before he let out a low growl once more. It seemed her bear liked it when she did that. Her arm still throbbed, but the pulsing of her clit, and the need burning inside her overshadowed the pain.

He let out another rumble as his tongue thrust again, and Jess cried out as she came. The breath froze in her lungs and everything went quiet and still. It was like the world fell away. As it all came into focus again, she felt the rasp of his tongue across the nipple she still pinched between her fingers. She gasped and watched, the sight erotic and sending another flash of heat straight to her aching pussy.

Tavish pressed his lips to hers, giving her a taste of her release before he drew away and stripped off his clothes. She'd known he was a big man, but the cock that jutted from the nest of hair between his legs was more than that. It was massive, and she felt her inner muscles clench in anticipation. Tavish reached down, giving the thick shaft a stroke as he watched her.

Jess licked her lips and brought her knees up so her feet were flat on the bed. She saw his fangs again as he snarled a little at her display. Jess cupped her breasts and teased her nipples. Tavish yanked on his cock harder and faster before abruptly stopping.

"Roll o'er, lass. You dinnae want me helpin' you get into position. I'll nae be gentle right now. My bear is tryin' to break free."

She flipped to her hands and knees, wincing as she put pressure on her arm. Tavish yanked her hips until her feet went to the floor, and he pressed her chest to the bed. She flattened her arms out, holding them above her head, while Tavish tipped her ass further up, sending her onto her tiptoes.

She felt the heat of his body settle over her, his chest to her back, his hips against her ass. And she felt the hard length of his cock slip between her legs, sliding against her slick pussy. With a flex of his hips, he started to work his cock inside her. She felt the burn as he stretched her wide. Jess wiggled a little, trying to keep purchase on the floor as her feet wanted to slide out from under her. Tavish snarled and pressed against her tighter, pinning her to the bed.

"Lass, I'd nae do that if I were you."

She started to slip again and shifted once more, drawing a fierce sound from her bear. He wrapped an arm around her waist, lifting her ass higher, and her feet left the floor. With his weight holding her to the mattress, Tavish thrust hard and deep, burying his cock inside her. Jess cried out in both shock and pleasure. But her bear was only just getting started.

He fucked her. It was the only way to describe it. It wasn't soft or sweet. It wasn't gentle or slow. It was a hard, thorough claiming as he slammed into her again and again. He angled his hips and on the next stroke hit just the right spot that made her see stars. When he did it again, her body started to tremble.

"Tavish, I… I… I think I'm going to…"

He didn't stop. His hips jerked against her. Two more strokes and she was screaming out her release. The shifter pinning her down sounded nearly feral as he took what he wanted. Had she been able to, she'd have lifted her ass higher, begging for more. His cock seemed to swell inside her and she felt a flash of red-hot pain in her shoulder as he bit down. It quickly turned to a different sort of heat, and another orgasm took her breath away.

Wave after wave of pleasure pulled her under. She shuddered under him and felt the hot splash of his cum as he filled her, every thrust driving it in deep. He snarled, his teeth still embedded in her. The hand braced on the bed got a fine sheen of brown fur for a moment before Tavish pulled his beast back.

Tavish released her and lapped at the wound on her shoulder. She felt a tingle, then a slight burn. He nuzzled her neck and nipped at her ear.

"I ken I should release you, mate, but I find I dinnae want to." He pressed his hips tighter to prove his point. "All soft and wet. You feel like heaven wrapped around my cock."

She felt him twitch inside her and noticed he hadn't softened. Was that a shifter thing? With Nicholas, sex had been quick, painful, and humiliating. She didn't think he'd actually wanted her in a sexual way, but seemed more to enjoy making her scream as he hurt her.

"Tavish, are you…"

He pulled back and thrust deep. "Hard? Aye, lass. I dinnae want to hurt you. Being human, you're more fragile, and already wounded."

"Maybe a different position?" she asked.

He released her, their mingled fluids sliding down her thigh. Tavish helped her onto her back, then gripped her wrists gently and placed them over her head.

"Keep them out of the way. I dinnae want to accidently hurt your arm."

She nodded and parted her thighs as he settled between them. He braced his weight on one arm as he leaned down, pressing their bodies together. His cock slid in far easier this time, and she moaned at how amazing he felt. How right. On the first stroke, her eyes went wide as he brushed her clit. Tavish winked at her and did it again, letting her know it had been on purpose. He drove her to distraction, teasing her and drawing out her pleasure. When he finally let her come, she felt hoarse from all the noise she'd been making.

Her bear came inside her twice more before he finally rolled to his side and pulled her with him. His cock remained sheathed in her pussy, with her leg over his hip. Tavish pressed a kiss to her forehead and sighed, a sound of pure contentment if ever she'd heard one.

"Ah, lass. You've made me the happiest bear. I finally have my mate where she belongs, in my bed." He thrust against her. "And on my cock."

She snorted and giggled. He reached up to unwrap the bandage on her arm and she realized it was already starting to heal. It no longer hurt, nor did her shoulder where he'd bitten her. If everyone knew about the perks of being mated to a shifter, they'd be lining up for a chance.

"Please stay safe, Tavish. Nicholas won't play fair. He'll do whatever it takes to make me miserable and cause me pain. And now that means he'll do his best to remove you from my life." There was a warmth in her chest, that spread through her body, when she thought of the bear holding her. "I feel... I..."

He brushed her nose with his. "It's the mate bond, lass. From my bite. Probably disnae hurt that you're also full of my cum."

She worried at her lip. "You want more children, right?"

"Aye. A house full."

"Good. Because I'm not on birth control."

He kissed her long and deep. "Ah, lass. I cannae wait for our cubs to arrive and show them their new home, let them shift and run on the property. And I cannae wait to see you swollen with our next cub."

She wanted that too. Just as soon as Nicholas was no longer a threat. She only hoped the bears could keep her and the children safe and put an end to their misery once and for all.

Chapter Seven

Tavish had made sure his new mate carried his scent. Once her arm had healed further, he'd taken her several more times. Now that he'd experienced what it was like to be in his mate's arms, he knew nothing he'd shared with anyone else could have ever compared. He didn't even remember those encounters now. Only the scent, sound, and taste of his mate. And he'd tasted her multiple times.

His damn bear had nearly broken free more than once, but he'd reined the beast in. Mostly. His vision had shifted during three different occasions, fur had sprouted along his hands and arms twice, and he'd felt his cock thicken every damn time he'd taken her. But she hadn't run from him. She'd just moaned sweetly and begged for more.

"Any word?" he asked Quinn.

"Calder caught a glimpse of him, but the coyote darted across the road, nearly getting hit by a car, before vanishing. He's a wily one." Quinn clapped him on the back. "We'll find him, Tavish. Focus on your family. You need to get two rooms ready for the cubs before they arrive."

"He broke into the house and attacked my mate. What if he gets in after the cubs arrive? He disnae seem to care who he hurts. If anythin', he enjoys inflictin' pain." If only he'd had a better grip when the coyote had shot past him after diving through the broken kitchen window. Taking a bite out of his hide had been a start, but he should have latched on tighter and finished it. He'd failed to protect his mate. "Might be time to involve the wolf pack."

"I'll stop and speak with them on my way to the pub. Keep to the house with your mate, Tavish. She needs you, and so does the clan." Quinn grinned. "I'm expendable, as the second son. And since you have a mate, you'll be havin' more cubs before long."

Tavish cuffed his brother on the head. "Gowk."

Quinn rubbed his head and flashed his alpha a smile. When Tavish was alone again, he wondered how he could flush out the coyote without using his mate or cubs as bait. He didn't understand why the shifter wanted Jessalyn so badly if they weren't true mates. Not to mention she said they'd married in the way humans did and had gotten a divorce. That certainly wasn't the way of any shifter he'd ever met. Coyotes were a troublesome lot, but Tavish started to think there was something more going on with Nicholas.

He heard voices and went to the staircase, waiting on his mate and her friends. Jessalyn gave him a bright smile as she hurried to him, wrapping her arms around his waist. Only mated one night, and already his soul felt complete with her by his side.

"I ken you came here on vacation, but with Nicholas still on the loose I have to insist you remain inside today. He managed to get onto the grounds once already, and into the house."

Jess ran her hand down his back. "I understand, Tavish, and so do my friends. After you've taken care of Nicholas, they can explore more. They want him gone just as much as you do, and while it's hard for all of them to adjust to shifters being real, I think they're handling it well. Only Monica knew about Nicholas being a shifter. We each have ways of keeping ourselves occupied. Don't feel like you have to fuss over us all day."

He kissed her softly. "Mate, there's nowhere else I'd rather be."

Monica sighed. "Guess it's too much to hope I'm a mate for one of your hunky brothers?"

Tavish smiled at her. "Sorry, lass. Only they would ken if you were. You saw my reaction to Jess at the pub. Have any of them fixated on you, insisted on takin' care of you?"

Monica sadly shook her head. "No. Damn it. All right, so no hunky bear shifter for me. Got it."

"What will the cubs need when they arrive? I'd like to prepare rooms for them in the family wing. I've nae been around teenage girls since I was that age myself." Tavish sighed. "I'll need to speak with the clan. Make sure no one tries anythin' with Piper."

"They won't be bringing a lot with them." Jess chewed on her lower lip. "Clothes and shoes, until the rest of their items can be shipped. Or it might be cheaper to just buy new stuff. Piper likes to read, so maybe some books. She likes dystopian stories. Donovan mostly plays video games."

"I'll ask Rhona to help get their rooms prepared. Any color preferences?" Tavish asked.

"Nothing overly girly for Piper. She loves purple. Other than that, she likes neutral tones mostly, and she hates frilly stuff. Donovan doesn't much care. As long as his bed is comfortable and he has a gaming system, he's usually content no matter if the rest of the building is falling down around his ears. His dad doesn't live in the best location, but as long as Donovan can play video games, it doesn't seem to bother him."

"I'll put them in the same hall as our room, but nae too close." He winked at her. "Enjoy your day with your friends, lass. I'll be nearby if you need me."

He walked away before he was tempted to do something else, like toss her over his shoulder and carry her back to their bed. His bite would ensure she'd healed, even if he'd left her a bit sore after claiming her so thoroughly. But it didn't mean he should chain her to the bed for the next several days, no matter how appealing it sounded.

He found Rhona in the laundry room, folding sheets and towels. He put his arm around her shoulders, and she tensed, looking up at him with narrowed eyes.

"Tavish MacBride, you only try to sweeten me up when you need something."

He grinned. "Aye, but you'll enjoy this task. I need two rooms set up for the cubs."

He relayed the information Jessalyn had given him about their likes and dislikes. He saw the gleam in her eyes as she thought about buying things for Piper. She'd always wanted girls to fuss over, and now she'd have her chance. Although Rhona wasn't technically family, she was still a part of their household and he loved her nearly as much as he loved his mother.

"Spending limits?" Rhona asked.

"Put everythin' on my account. Just leave the receipts on my desk in case we need to return anythin'." He hesitated. "Perhaps let the cubs' new uncles help pick out the items for Donovan's room. They might actually enjoy it."

Rhona gave a nod, then turned back to the laundry. He knew once she'd finished, she'd leave to run her errands. As much as Tavish wanted to pick out Donovan's things himself, Quinn had been correct about him staying home today. It wasn't safe for his mate to leave home, and he wasn't about to run off without her. Not when Nicholas could strike again when they least expected it. The nasty coyote couldn't be dealt with soon enough.

He called Quinn to see how things had gone with

the Murdochs. His brother didn't answer, so Tavish hung up and dialed again, this time catching his brother on the third ring. His brother grunted a greeting as he picked up.

"Will they help?" Tavish asked.

"Aye. They will. In fact, one of them saw the hurdie an hour ago. They're trackin' his scent and hope to have a lock on him soon. I'll call when I hear somethin'."

"Calder with you?"

"He's trackin' Nicholas as well. Did you need him?"

"Donovan likes video games. I need a console and some games a thirteen-year-old shifter might like. One who's afraid of turnin' out like his father."

Quinn growled softly. "You're the boy's father. The other is only a sperm donor. But I'll see it's done. If I cannae get to the store, I'll ask Gavan to handle it. Anythin' else?"

"Clothes, but I dinnae ken what sizes. I'll have to ask Jess and get back to you."

"Just text me, Tavish. I'll be sure to check before I buy anything. Right now, I'm trying to corner Nicholas before he can do any more damage. How's your mate?"

"Healed, mostly. The gouges were deep, but the skin is already knittin' together. She may scar."

"Do you care if she has scars?" Quinn asked.

"It's nae the scars so much as the reminder. Every time she sees them, she'll remember her fear when he attacked her, and possibly remember every other time he caused her pain. I wish I could wipe him from her memory altogether. He disnae deserve even a second of her attention."

"Agreed," Quinn said. "Go find out the boy's

sizes and I'll pick up some things. And Tavish, I dinnae have to tell you how blessed you are. Enjoy your mate, brother. If anyone deserves a family, it's you."

His brother's words warmed his heart.

Jessalyn and her friends were scattered across couches in the main room. His mate had curled into the corner of one and had a book in her hand. It seemed his new daughter had taken after her mother, since Jess had informed him Piper liked to read. He paused in the doorway, watching her. A warmth spread through his chest. It had felt, at times, like he'd never find his destined mate. And now she was here, in his home, in his bed… Whatever it took, he'd keep her safe.

He approached his mate and knelt in front of her. "Lass, I'm sendin' two people out for items for the cubs. I need clothin' and shoe sizes. I want them to feel at home when they arrive."

Jess gave him a sweet smile before answering him, then leaned forward and brushed her lips against his. Tavish gave a low growl and he felt his bear rising to the surface. Already the randy beast wanted her again. The scent of her arousal filled the air, and he knew if he didn't walk away right then, he really would toss her over his shoulder and carry her back to their room.

He gripped the back of her neck and gave her a more thorough kiss before he quickly left. He sent his brother a message about Donovan's sizes, made sure Rhona knew what to get Piper, then decided to see what he could discover about his mate's ex-husband. Knowing the man was a coyote shifter and violent toward Jess and the cubs wasn't enough. If there was another way to get to him, to keep him in line, Tavish wanted to know.

He called the local alpha of the wolf pack. With

the man's law enforcement connections, if anyone could sniff out dirt on Nicholas it would be Seamus Murdoch.

The wolf answered with a growl. "I'm busy."

"Apologies, Alpha, but I need your help."

The man was quiet a moment. "Tavish MacBride?"

"Aye."

The wolf signed. "Fine. What is it?"

"My mate's ex, the coyote your clan is searchin' for, seems even more unbalanced than I'd expect from one of his ilk. I need to find out more about him. There has to be another way to beat him into submission. If we cannae do it physically, as the bawbag keep evading capture, then maybe we can hurt him in other ways."

"I'll see what I can dig up and call you back." The wolf hung up without another word.

Tavish felt his bear rising under the surface, needing to come out. He went out onto the back veranda and stripped down before shifting into his beast. With a roar, he charged down the stairs and across his land. He'd patrol the area near the house, up to the tree line, and make sure no one had entered his property without permission. His paws dug into the ground, his claws sinking into the earth as he propelled himself forward. He scented the air, ensuring the coyote hadn't returned.

As he neared the woods on the other side of the house, he paused. His nose twitched and he took a deeper pull of the air. A familiar scent, but one that shouldn't be present. Annis. He'd known the woman would be trouble when he'd spurned her, but he didn't like the fact she was so close to his mate. He growled and searched her out. He heard a giggle, then a manly groan. Tavish stopped, mid-step and scented the air again. Who did Annis come to see? As far as he knew, his brothers were all off searching for Nicholas.

He sniffed again and crept closer, moving as soundlessly as possible. He saw the flash of her hair near a tree just inside the wooded line. Tavish moved behind a tree, easing further into the shadows. As he got closer to the pair, the man's scent hit Tavish, making him fight not to sneeze. He'd doused himself in cologne, which told Tavish the man wanted to hide his scent. There would only be one reason to do something like that.

He heard the clink of a belt and the rasp of a zipper. "Promise you'll do whatever I demand?"

"I'll do anythin' you want," Annis said, her voice a near purr.

"Anything?" the man asked. His voice made Tavish's fur stand up.

"Yes," she said.

"Strip," the man said.

Tavish heard the rustle of her clothes. He couldn't get closer without bringing attention to himself. Not that he cared about seeing Annis naked, but it was curious she'd met the man on his lands. Why were they here?

"You're sure everyone knows you've been seeing the bear?" the man asked.

Tavish held back a growl.

"Aye. We've been a couple for a bit. Until he ended things recently." He heard her moan. "But he's nae the man you are, Nicky."

Nicky? As in Nicholas? His mate's ex-husband? He didn't know what the man was up to, but Tavish had a bad feeling about the two of them being on his lands. He needed to call the Murdoch alpha, in case things went sideway, but he didn't exactly carry a phone with him as a bear.

The grunts of them having sex reached his ears and he dared to get closer. Nicholas had Annis's face shoved hard into the ground, a fistful of her hair in his hand, as he fucked her from behind. His claw-tipped fingers broke the skin on her hip as he took her roughly. She whimpered and writhed under him.

"Yes! Just like that, Nicky."

The coyote wrenched her head back and snarled at her, saliva dripping from his fangs. "Shut it, whore. You don't make demands."

He suddenly pulled out, then thrust into Annis's ass, making her squeal and buck, this time in pain. He held her down, using her as he saw fit. Tavish wanted to intervene, but her next words held him in place.

"Do it, Nicky. Make it hurt."

When the coyote finished, he slashed his claws across her back multiple times before flipping her over and shredding the skin across her breasts. Annis paled and bit her lip hard enough it bled. Somehow, she kept from screaming. He backed off, leaving her a bloody mess. "And what will you say when you stumble out of here like that?"

"That Tavish hurt me," she said, giving him a smile. She eyed the man's cock, which hadn't softened. "But I think it's you who wants to hurt me some more."

"You're right. I do. I want to fuck you, use you, make you scream in pain." He licked his lips. "But first I want to kill my whore of an ex-wife. When she's gone, I'll give you everything you want and what I need. Now go. Make sure it's a good performance."

Tavish spun and dashed back toward his home. He didn't bother dressing before grabbing his phone and calling the Murdoch alpha to let him know everything he'd seen and heard. By the time Annis made her appearance, blubbering about Tavish trying to kill her, the local police would know the truth. Instead of Tavish being hauled away in handcuffs, the hunt for Nicholas doubled. Sooner or later, the coyote's luck would run out.

Chapter Eight

Jessalyn felt herself pale when Tavish explained what he'd seen and heard. She'd known Nicholas was brutal and thrived on causing pain, but she hadn't realized the extent of his depravity. To be truthful, she'd heard whispers that he liked to fuck women while in his shifted form, causing far more damage than he'd done to the woman who'd tried to frame Tavish. She just hadn't wanted to believe it.

"What now?" she asked.

"You keep to the castle," Tavish said. "Everyone is searchin' for Nicholas. It wilnae be long now, lass. He can only run for so far, unless he returns to the States."

"Tavish, what about the kids? While you were gone, I spoke with my mother. She said their flight gets in tomorrow. That's only one day to get Nicholas under control. What if it's not enough?"

He took her hand and gave it a squeeze. "Lass, I'll nae let him harm you or the cubs. I'll do whatever it takes to keep you safe."

"He won't stop. I don't know why he wants me, or rather why he enjoys hurting me so much. He's never loved me. I'd hoped when I got the divorce, maybe he'd finally move on."

Tavish cupped her cheeks. "It's nae you. He's twisted and his mind is broken. Coyotes are a nasty lot most of the time, but Nicholas is worse than any I've seen. If Annis haednae been useful to him, he'd likely have killed her and enjoyed it. For him, it was sexual, lass. He got off on the pain he caused, enjoyed the bloodshed. The way he spoke of killin' you… it's nae right."

A throat cleared behind them and Jess turned her

head, seeing one of Tavish's brothers. Dirt and grass clung to him. His shirt looked torn, and there was a nasty set of claw marks down his cheek.

"Calder, what happened?" Tavish asked.

"I found the coyote," he said. His gaze shifted to Jess. "I caught him, though he didnae go easy. You'll be safe now, and so will the cubs. The Murdochs have him in custody."

"He's at the police station?" she asked.

Calder's lips twitched as if he fought back a grin. "Nae exactly. They're waitin' on Tavish, on Murdoch lands. The coyote is bein' held in the old barn. As your mate, it's Tavish's right to get justice for the pain Nicholas caused."

Tavish growled. "Aye. I'll gladly mete out his punishment."

Jess tugged on his hand. "I want to go too."

Tavish shook his head. "It's nae safe, lass. Nor a place you should be. There will be bloodshed."

She jutted her chin out and firmed her jaw. "Good. I need to see him pay, Tavish. For every slap, punch, broken bone… for the fear I've lived with all these years, and the way he made my children suffer. I need to watch as he breathes his last, because I know damn well you're going to kill him, and I'm all right with that. I came to terms long ago with the fact some people will never change. There are monsters in the world who need to be destroyed, and Nicholas is one of them."

Tavish leaned down and kissed her soft and slow. "Aye, lass. You can come. But nae if you're goin' to interfere. You stay back and let me handle the bawbag."

She'd have promised anything if it meant seeing for herself that Nicholas could no longer hurt her.

She'd be able to stop jumping at shadows. It had been too long since she'd felt safe even in her own home. Changing continents hadn't helped. He'd followed her. The only way to end it all would be to kill Nicholas. But hearing it was done and seeing his lifeless body were two different things. She'd changed over the years. The Jessalyn she'd been when she'd met Nicholas would have never wanted to see a man die. Then he'd slowly killed that woman, and someone different had risen in her place.

"I'll do whatever you say, Tavish. I just need to be there."

"I'll stay by her side," Calder said. "It would be an honor."

Tavish gave a nod and helped Jess to her feet. They went out to his truck and the three of them drove to the barn where Nicholas was waiting. Or rather, they drove to a gate and then walked the rest of the way on foot. The barn was easily a mile from the fence line, but Jess didn't think anyone would bat an eye at any screams or sounds of pain coming from the Murdochs' land, not after the entire town had been asked about Nicholas.

Yet Jessalyn couldn't help but wonder if one person in town had sided with Nicholas, could others do the same? Tavish had assured her, despite Annis's agreement with Nicholas, no one else wanted the coyote around. Everyone had gladly helped keep an eye out for him and notified the MacBrides whenever he'd been spotted. Thankfully, it would finally be over, and Jess could start her new life with Tavish and the kids. She hoped they never asked about their father. If they did, she'd simply say he was gone and never coming back. Maybe when they were older, she'd tell them the truth. Even though Piper was only two years shy of being an adult, she wasn't ready to watch her daughter grow up any sooner than she had to.

Jessalyn stepped inside the barn, keeping close to the door with Calder by her side. Tavish approached Nicholas. The coyote sneered at him before fastening his hateful gaze on her. Jess shivered, but she refused to back down. She needed to see this through to the end, not just for herself. She needed to do it for her children.

Her ex had been bound to a metal chair with chains. His ankles had been shackled and attached to large rings in the hard-packed ground. Despite how rough Calder looked, it was clear her ex had taken quite the beating.

"How does it feel to be the one bloody and broken?" she asked.

Nicholas stared at her without saying a word. When he looked at Tavish, she knew something hateful would come out of his mouth.

"How's it feel to be mated to a whore? To know I had her first? Fucked her any way I wanted, as often as I wanted? Got her pregnant twice?"

Tavish growled and Jess watched as his hand shifted into a large bear paw. "I'd thought to draw this out a bit. I can see it wouldnae make a difference. The world will be a better place without you in it."

The coyote laughed, madness lurking in his eyes. It was clear he'd come completely unhinged. Jess didn't know how she hadn't seen it before. Or maybe she'd been too afraid to look too closely at her ex-husband. How long had he hidden the insanity she could so clearly see now? She glanced at Tavish, hoping he understood that she needed answers.

"Why? Why come after her now?" Tavish asked.

The coyote's eyes glowed and saliva dripped

from his fangs as he snarled. "Because it's her fault. All of it."

"What's my fault?" Jess asked.

"She died. Because of you," Nicholas said.

"She?" Tavish asked.

"My mate." A flash of pain crossed the coyote's face. "She couldn't handle me anymore. I used the human to let out some of the aggression. My own little punching bag. It was enough that my mate didn't get too badly injured when we were together."

Jessalyn felt her eyes go wide when Tavish looked her way. There'd been another woman? And a mate? If he'd found his true mate, why had he bothered to marry *her*? For that matter, how had he borne being able to touch her, to be intimate with her and have children? From what little she'd learned so far, it should have been nearly impossible for him to do such a thing if he were mated.

"You had a mate?" Jess asked. "Even before you married me?"

He snarled again. "Yes. But she was… broken. In her mind. I had to keep her somewhere safe. No one could know about her. Everything was fine, until you left and filed for divorce. I found others, but it wasn't the same. I needed that daily outlet to keep me from hurting her too much."

Quinn took a step closer. "You had a mate locked up somewhere. How could you hurt her? Even if you didn't have Jess and the kids anymore, it goes against everything we are to hurt our true mates."

The coyote closed his eyes, pain etched across his features. "Because I'm broken too."

"He's mad, Tavish," Quinn said. "The kind you don't come back from. His mind is too badly damaged. Nothing will stop him from wanting to hurt Jess and the kids. He's… feral."

Tavish nodded in agreement. "Aye, and there's only one thing to do when a shifter goes feral."

He lashed out, drawing his claws down both sides of Nicholas's face, making him scream in pain. Her mate slashed at his arms, chest and abdomen, before finally raking his claws across the coyote's throat, making the shifter choke on his own blood. Jess made herself witness her ex draw his last breath. She moved closer, staying far enough back from the blood spatter, but near enough she could see his cold, dead eyes… the life drained from them.

"I'm finally free," she whispered.

"Aye, lass." Tavish tipped his head and studied her. "He'll nae bother anyone again."

Calder grunted. "Rather anti-climactic. I'd have made him suffer more."

Tavish cast his brother a glare, but remained silent.

"I'll dispose of the body," someone said, drawing closer. "Take your mate home, Tavish. Put this nastiness behind you."

Tavish looked at his hand, now human once more but covered in blood. He went over to a barrel and dipped his hand inside, then pulled it out and shook off the excess water. He still wouldn't touch her, and while Jess appreciated the gesture, she wasn't worried about getting her clothes dirty. She flung her arms around his waist and snuggled in.

"Thank you, Tavish. Not just for what you did today, but for everything. I'd started to think men like you didn't exist except in fairy tales."

"I'm nae perfect, lass." He ran a hand down her hair. "But I'd do anythin' for you. You're my mate, Jessalyn. The other half of my soul. For you, I'd pull down the heavens, lay down my life, or vanquish any and all evil that tries to take you from me."

Calder snorted as he walked over. "Layin' it on thick. Next you'll be writin' sonnets."

Tavish narrowed his eyes at his brother before cuffing him on the back of the head. "Awa' and bile yer heid."

She blinked up at him. "Do I even want to know what that means?"

"He told me to get lost," Calder said with a smirk. "I'll be headin' home now. Need to clean up and let Rhona fuss over me."

Tavish huffed, but Jess saw the affection in his eyes when he looked at his brother. She'd never had brothers, but it seemed she was inheriting a family by being with Tavish. Now she'd have three brothers like she'd always wanted though she loved her sister and would miss her. Once her friends were gone she'd have no one here to gossip with, no one to fix her hair or laugh over the latest romantic comedy with. With some luck, she'd convince Cherise to come visit. And if not, maybe Tavish would take them to the US once a year.

"Come, mate." Tavish led her out of the barn. When she'd finally broken free of Nicholas, or at least tried, she'd thought she was finished with shifters. Now she'd moved to Scotland, mated a bear, and lived in a town that also had werewolves. It just proved that life could easily change in unexpected ways.

Tavish shifted his weight as he climbed into the truck, a grimace crossing his face. She opened her mouth to ask if he'd been hurt, but her cheeks warmed when she realized the problem. It seemed her bear wanted to get home for one specific reason, and the evidence was tenting his kilt. After his very thorough claiming, she couldn't deny she looked forward to being intimate with him again. She'd never known anyone like him before.

The ride home was quiet. Tavish's knuckles were white as he gripped the steering wheel. He didn't so much as look her way, but his nostrils flared with every inhale, as if he were taking in her scent. Jess pressed her thighs together, feeling an ache building inside her. A soft growl came from her bear.

"If you dinnae want to be mauled on the side of the road, lass, I suggest you think of somethin' else. Anythin' else." Her clit swelled and pulsed with need, making Tavish groan. "I cannae take much more, Jess. Your scent… it's incredible."

They managed to make it home, and Tavish practically dove from the truck, lifting Jess into his arms and carrying her inside. He took the stairs two at a time as he raced to their room. She giggled when he kicked the door shut and tossed her onto the bed. She bounced before settling on her back.

"Strip, mate. I need you."

"Tavish, a water barrel didn't get you clean enough. Hugging you while covered in blood is one thing. Don't even think of doing more than that until you've scrubbed all of Nicholas off you."

He flashed his fangs at her, but he went into the adjoining bath and she heard the shower start. Jess stripped out of her clothes and decided to join her bear. The water cascaded over his body, and she couldn't help but lick her lips. The man was a work of art. She stepped into the shower stall, placing her hands against his back.

Tavish spun and lifted her, pressing her against the wall. He held her in place by pinning his hips against hers. She felt his cock nestle between her thighs, the heat branding her pussy.

"Tavish," she said, his name a near whisper as she ran her fingers across his jaw.

His eyes turned golden and he snarled a little. "I'll make it up to you, Jess. I'm sorry."

She didn't get a chance to ask what he meant before he thrust hard and deep. She gasped and closed her eyes, her nails biting into his shoulders as he powered into her again and again. Her orgasm rushed through her like a tidal wave. The pleasure didn't get a chance to wane before she was flying again. Tavish made her come three times before he bellowed, and the hot spurts of his release filled her.

Her lips crashed against his and she fisted his hair as she held on. "My crazy, protective bear. What did I ever do to deserve you?"

"I was wonderin' the same, lass, because you're an angel and I've been a very bad bear." He winked. "And I plan to be bad again."

He started thrusting once more and soon she was whimpering and begging for more. Whatever the future brought, as long as she had Tavish by her side, she knew it would all work out. He was the best thing to happen to her, other than her kids. And the insane sex was a bonus.

By the time he gave her a reprieve, she ached in the best of ways. With a smile on her face, she helped prepare for the arrival of her children, and hoped they'd be as happy with their new lives as she was with hers. More importantly, she really wanted them to give Tavish a chance.

Chapter Nine

Tavish stood with his hands braced behind his back. He'd let Jess pick up the children at the airport with Rhona. He watched out the lower-level windows, waiting for her to return. When the truck pulled in, he fought the urge to rush to her side. His bear was anxious to meet the cubs. After all they'd suffered, he didn't know if they'd accept another shifter into their family. If Jess hadn't been so badly injured, he'd have waited to mate her. Now, whether the cubs liked him or not, they would live together. He'd never let his mate go.

"Tavish!"

He turned to face her and the cubs. They watched him uncertainly, and he made sure to move slow as he walked toward them. Donovan stared up at him with wide eyes. Even though the cub was technically a teenager, his stature was slight compared to Tavish's. The boy stood nearly as tall as his mother. Piper was smaller and a little on the plump side, but Tavish found her rather adorable even with a slight scowl on her face.

"Did you have a good flight?" he asked them.

"It was okay," Piper said.

"They called their grandparents when we got in the car to let them know they'd made it safely. I think they're already a little homesick." Jess ruffled Donovan's hair. "I've told them how beautiful this place is and how eager everyone is to meet them."

"Rhona and Cook are preparing something special for tonight," Tavish said. "A few local specialties, as well as a homemade pizza, which your mom assured me is your favorite."

"Are you really a bear?" Piper asked.

"Aye. Can you nae tell?" She shook her head. Tavish leaned in a little closer. "Take a sniff, little cub. Then smell your mom and see if you can tell the difference."

Piper breathed him in and wrinkled her nose before scenting her mother. "You smell musky compared to her."

"Aye. Because I'm a bear and she's a human. You'll have a chance to sniff other shifters and learn how to spot them. Even if you're meeting a shifter for the first time, you should be able to tell by scent what they are. It's nae hard to learn, and we have time."

Both kids shared a look that seemed to be a mix of confusion and hope. He wondered if Nicholas had tried to crush their beasts' spirits. It seemed he'd done his best to not teach the cubs anything about their true selves, and they knew nothing of their instincts or abilities. Most fathers would have enjoyed teaching their cubs about their heritage and what it meant to be a shifter, but then the coyote hadn't acted like a normal shifter. He'd been too damaged to function properly, and should have been put down long ago.

Tavish gave her a smile. "Ready to see your new home?"

They looked at their mom and she gave them a nod of encouragement. "Tavish worked hard to make sure you'd have your own rooms, and some new things. He wants you to be happy here."

The boy's jaw tightened, and his eyes narrowed. "I'm not going to let you hurt my mom."

Tavish took a breath and went down on one knee so he could look Donovan in the eye at his level. "I'd never hurt your mom. She's my mate, which means she, and you, are the most important people in my life. I would die for her."

The kids shared a look.

Jessalyn put her hands on their shoulders. "Remember how I said your dad wouldn't be a problem anymore? That's because of Tavish. He made sure we'd be safe here. When he said he'd die for us, he meant it. He's an honorable man, and I hope you'll give him a chance."

Piper's stance eased a bit. "Is my room purple?"

Tavish grinned. "Your uncle Quinn painted it lavender just for you. Ready to see it?"

She nodded and he led the way up to the family wing. Their footsteps echoed in the otherwise silent castle. Everyone else had made themselves scarce so they wouldn't overwhelm the kids. Although Tavish wouldn't have minded his mother's presence at the moment. He'd expected her to be a bit more involved since he'd finally found his mate, but she'd given them space. Most likely because his mate was human and had needed time to adjust. Despite the fact Jessalyn had married a shifter, the experience had been rough. She'd learned to trust his family, and they'd formed a strong bond. He hoped his mother would realize she was still needed even though Jessalyn was technically the lady of the castle now.

Tavish pushed open the door to Piper's room and the girl hesitantly stepped inside. When he heard her gasp, he noticed her eyes were brighter than before. A soft smile curved her lips and she turned to fling her arms around him.

"Thank you! It's perfect!"

The scowl on Donovan's face eased a little. "Can I see mine?"

"Aye," Tavish said, leading the cub to his room. He heard Piper squeal after she flung open the wardrobe and knew she'd found her new clothes and shoes.

Donovan stepped into the gray bedroom and looked around. Since Jess had said the boy was into gaming, they'd hung posters from what he'd been assured were popular video games. There were two systems hooked up to a TV with an armchair nearby for comfort while he played. To further offset the pale gray walls, his brother had picked out a navy blanket for the bed.

Donovan turned to face him. Any tension had eased from the cub as he tipped his head to the side to watch Tavish. He waited, having enough patience for the cub to gather his thoughts.

"You're different from him, aren't you?" Donovan asked.

"Aye. Nae all shifters like to cause pain. You should ken that already, since you're one too."

Donovan's lips twisted and he cast his gaze down. "I don't want to be like him."

"You wilnae be anythin' like Nicholas. The fact you're worried about turning out as rotten as your father means you'll work hard to be a good man. This town has bears and wolves to teach you how to be strong and fierce, yet keep a gentle touch with those under your protection. Like your mother and sister."

Donovan nodded. "I think I'd like that. I've been scared every time I've shifted and try hard not to. It would be nice to run as my beast without fearing I'll hurt someone."

"We'll work on it, lad. Your new uncles are eager to teach you everythin' and anythin'. All you have to do is ask."

He smiled then. "Uncles? I haven't had those before."

"Aye. And you have a new grandmother too.

You'll meet her shortly." Tavish moved closer. "I'm nae tryin' to replace your family, Donovan. I'm only expandin' it a bit. Your mother's family is welcome here any time they wish. And I'm nae trying to replace your father. I ken he wasnae the sort you want to emulate, but he was blood just the same."

Donovan moved over to the bed and sank onto the side of it. "He beat us. All of us. He'd use me and Piper to control Mom and keep her under his thumb. When he'd make her, or us, cry, he'd laugh. He enjoyed hurting people. Especially Piper, after he found out she wasn't a coyote."

"Aye, your mom told me about it. I bet she's an adorable platypus."

"You'll let her shift?" Donovan asked. "Even after you see her beast? Our other dad got angry when she shifted."

"Of course! In fact, would you like to shift and explore the property a bit? Near the castle, though. Until the fence has been repaired, and I'm certain no danger lurks on our lands, I dinnae want you wanderin' far."

His eyes lit up and he nodded eagerly.

"Then let's get your sister."

Donovan raced to his sister's room and immediately told her about Tavish's idea to shift and explore. Once she learned he didn't dislike her animal form, both his new cubs were eager to go outside. Jess held his hand as they walked to the back veranda. As the cubs stripped and shifted, Tavish leaned down to kiss his mate.

"Thank you, lass. You've given me everythin' I ever wanted. A family."

"You've given us a safe place and have shown me how a man should treat a woman. Tavish, if anyone is thankful, it's me. I know we haven't been together more than a few days, but you've already changed my life." She kissed him again. "I love you."

Tavish wrapped an arm around her waist, hauling her against him, and kissed her like a starving man. Hearing those three words made this the best moment of his life. He had a mate who loved him. Tavish couldn't think of anything more important than that. She'd blessed him by coming here, giving him a chance. Whatever it took, he'd make sure she never regretted her decision. As a shifter, he'd known she was meant to be his from the start, but as a human she'd not had the same instincts to trust, or sense of smell. It humbled Tavish that she could accept him as her mate, especially after all she'd suffered.

"I love you, lass. More than anythin'."

With one last kiss, he stripped and shifted, then went to play with his cubs. And he'd been right, Piper was an adorable platypus.

Epilogue

Six Months Later

Jess rubbed at her lower back and winced as her muscles tightened even further. Her feet were swollen, even though she'd had them propped up the last hour. If it weren't for her bladder screaming at her to move, she'd have gladly stayed in her chair a while longer. She managed to haul herself upright and made the trek to the bathroom.

"And what are you doing up?"

Jess froze and slowly turned to face her mother-in-law. "I had to pee."

Mother MacBride, as Jess had been instructed to call her, clucked her tongue. "You should have called for someone, lass."

Jess placed a hand on her belly. "I'm pregnant, not an invalid."

"Aye. Pregnant with twin bear cubs. And large ones from what I can see. Did you nae say you weren't even this big full-term with your first two?"

"You're right, Mother MacBride. I'll try to remember to ask for help. I'm still not used to having people around I can rely on, but I'll do better."

Her mother-in-law kissed her cheek, then helped her back to the chair once she'd used the restroom. She looked out the window to her right and smiled as she watched her mate and cubs romp through the grass in their animal forms. Donovan had already become a much stronger boy, not just physically but mentally and emotionally. He adored his new father, but stuck to his uncles like glue most days. Piper had blossomed nearly overnight. She smiled more and seemed genuinely happy for the first time that Jess could remember.

Her phone rang and she picked it up.

"Hi, Monica. How's mated life treating you?" she asked.

Her friend squealed. "It's amazing! Why didn't you tell me how great shifter sex was? Oh my God! Seamus is just so… so…"

"I get it," Jess said.

Monica had met the alpha wolf right before she'd planned to return home six months ago. Instead, she'd stayed another week to get to know the wolf better. Since then, she'd returned twice and the last time decided to stay. She'd officially mated the older man three days ago, their age difference not seeming to bother her.

"If Seamus has it his way, I'll have a son or daughter who can grow up playing with your two youngest. He's doing his best to knock me up."

Jess heard the rumble of Seamus Murdoch's voice in the background. "And what do his children think of their new stepmom who's near their age?"

"Honestly, they don't care. True mates are apparently rare, so they're thrilled for us. Anyway, I just wanted to check in and say hi. It seems I'm needed again. Call me in a few days and we'll get together for lunch."

Jess smiled. "Enjoy your honeymoon."

She set the phone aside and watched her family through the window again, running her hand over her stomach. "It won't be long before the two of you will want to shift and play too, then your mom will be the only human stuck inside."

"It's nae that bad, is it?" Quinn asked as he entered the room.

"No. I love it here, and I love all of you. I just feel like the odd woman out sometimes."

"Then I guess one of us will have to mate a human," he said.

Jessalyn waved her hand at him. "As if you have any intention of settling down anytime soon. You enjoy being single and having your pick of the ladies, and don't bother denying it."

Quinn sighed. "Aye, I do. But one day it wilnae be enough. Deep down, we all want our mates, lass. I'll enjoy my freedom while I have it, but once I find my mate, I wilnae miss my days as a bachelor. I want what you and Tavish have. Maybe nae right now, but someday soon."

"You'll find her, Quinn. Probably when you least expect it."

He settled into the chair across from hers. "Now, what shall we do to pass the time until your cubs are worn out and ready to be on two legs again?"

"Something that doesn't require me to move?" she asked.

"All right. What's that game Donovan wanted to play last week? Ah. I spy something that's red."

Jess's lips twitched. "That's not entirely how that line goes, but close enough."

She spent the next twenty minutes playing the game with Quinn, until her mate and cubs came back inside. Then her handsome bear carried her to their room and reminded her exactly how she'd gotten to be the size of a small whale. And she adored every second of it.

She'd traveled across an ocean before she'd discovered what love was, but now she had a sweet, sexy mate and a big family. The only way life could be more perfect was if she could convince her sister and parents to move, but they insisted on remaining in the US. One day she'd change their minds. Until then, she'd make lots of happy memories, take a ton of pictures, and live life to the fullest.

"Love you, Baloo," she murmured before kissing him.

"I'm nae a cartoon bear."

She smiled. "No. You're my big, bad bear in plaid. And you're absolutely perfect for me just the way you are."

Dear Reader

Thank you for reading Mad, Bad Bear! We hope you enjoyed the story. If you have a moment, we'd be grateful if you'd leave a rating or review at the bookseller of your choice, Goodreads, or BookBub to let other readers know what you loved or didn't like about this novella.

We tried to make this story as light as possible, even though it does touch on darker subjects. Domestic violence is a serious issue and far too common a problem. Jessalyn's guilt for staying, and her feeling of helplessness over not being able to leave sooner, may not be how each survivor feels. Everyone is different, and each situation is unique. The portrayal of her character in no way is meant to represent everyone who's been in that position before, and we hope it didn't offend anyone.

Thank you for your support!

Jessica & Kenna

Scottish Slang Cheat Sheet

Amnae -- am not

Arenae -- are not

Awa' and bile yer heid -- Get lost

Aye -- yes

Bampot -- Idiot

Baw -- testicle (bawbag is an insult)

Brae/s -- hill/s

Cannae - cannot

Didnae -- did not

Dinnae -- don't

Disnae -- Doesn't

Get it right up ye -- fuck right off

Gowk -- fool/simpleton

Haednae -- hadn't

Hurdie -- asshole

Havnae -- have not

Ken -- understand

Mo ghradh -- my love

Nae -- No/Not

Wouldnae -- would not

Wernae -- were not

Wee -- little or small

Wheesht -- be silent

Wilnae -- won't

Wasnae -- was not

Kenna McKay

Kenna McKay is a lover of all things Scottish -- especially men in kilts! There's just something sexy about Scotsmen. The Scottish burr, perhaps? Their rugged good looks? Maybe it's not just one thing, but everything combined into one mouthwatering package.

Kenna didn't start out wanting to be a writer, but she's loved the written word for as long as she can remember. Writing stories from a young age, it wasn't until 2014 that she decided she wanted to be a published author.

Kenna at Changeling: changelingpress.com/kenna-mckay-a-219

Jessica Coulter Smith

Award-winning author Jessica Coulter Smith has been in love with the written word since she was a child writing her first stories in crayon. Today she's a multi-published author of over seventy-five novellas and novels. Romance is an integral part of her world and she firmly believes that love will find you at the right time, even if Mr. Right is literally out of this world.

Jessica at Changeling: changelingpress.com/jessica-coulter-smith-a-144

Changeling Press E-Books

More Sci-Fi, Fantasy, Paranormal, and BDSM adventures available in e-book format for immediate download at ChangelingPress.com -- Werewolves, Vampires, Dragons, Shapeshifters and more -- Erotic Tales from the edge of your imagination.

What are E-Books?

E-books, or electronic books, are books designed to be read in digital format -- on your desktop or laptop computer, notebook, tablet, Smart Phone, or any electronic e-book reader.

Where can I get Changeling Press E-Books?

Changeling Press e-books are available at ChangelingPress.com, Amazon, Apple Books, Barnes & Noble, and Kobo/Walmart.